The Ghosts of Magnificent Children

Caroline Busher

POOLBEG

Published 2016
by Poolbeg Press Ltd
123 Grange Hill, Baldoyle
Dublin 13, Ireland
E-mail: poolbeg@poolbeg.com

© CAROLINE BUSHER 2016

The moral right of the author has been asserted.

Typesetting, editing, layout, design, ebook © Poolbeg Press Ltd.

1

A catalogue record for this book is available from the British Library.

ISBN 978-1-78199-874-8

Author cover photo by John Busher
Typeset by Poolbeg

Printed and bound by CPI Group (UK) Ltd, Croydon, CR0 4YY

www.poolbeg.com

The Ghosts of Magnificent Children

About the Author

Caroline Busher graduated with a First Class Honours MA in Creative Writing from UCD. She grew up in a Victorian house in the North-west of England. As an only child Caroline spent her days reading books and writing fantastical stories. When she got older she moved to the South-east of Ireland where she now lives with her husband John and her children Fiachra, Caoimhe and Tiernan. Caroline strongly believes that it is the most magical place on earth. Her house is nestled beneath the Blackstairs Mountains. But be warned: if you ever go there you must tread carefully. The mountains resemble sleeping giants and legend has it that the giants might wake up someday.

Caroline is the recipient of two literature awards from Wexford County Council and Artlinks. She was highly commended in the Cross Pens/Writing.ie Short Story Competition, longlisted for the Penguin Ireland Short Story Competition, published as part of the RTÉ *100 Words/100 Books Competition* and shortlisted for Bord Gáis Energy Book Club/TV3 Short Story Award.

Caroline teaches creative writing courses to adults and children and is a curator for Wexford Literary Festival.

The Ghosts of Magnificent Children is Caroline's debut novel.

Acknowledgements

When I was a little girl my parents brought me to the circus. I was mesmerised by the ease with which the trapeze artists flew through the air, the death-defying tightrope-walkers and the beautiful women in sequinned costumes riding on horseback.

It was this childhood memory that inspired me to write *The Ghosts of Magnificent Children* but, just like a spectacular circus, a book cannot happen without the help and support of many wonderful people.

I am so grateful to my extraordinary agent Tracy Brennan. I could not have done it without you, Tracy. Thank you for believing in me and for getting my book into the right hands.

Thank you so much to everyone at Poolbeg Press, especially to Paula Campbell who made my dream of becoming a published author a reality, and to Gaye Shortland who is a skilled editor and an absolute pleasure to work with.

Sincere thanks to Wexford County Council Arts Department and to Artlinks for awarding me Literature Bursaries in 2014 and 2016. Your continued support of my practice has enabled me to develop my craft as a writer. Thank you to the Tyrone Guthrie Centre at Annaghmakerrig for the beautiful space to edit my work. I would also like to thank Wexford Library Services for all your hard work and for inviting me into your wonderful libraries to facilitate creative writing workshops.

Thanks to the UCD School of English, Drama and Film, and to the MA in Creative Writing Department. Thank you, James Ryan, Frank McGuinness, Paul Perry and Éilis Ní Dhuibhne.

I would like to say an extra special thank-you to Éilis Ní Dhuibhne for being my mentor whilst I was writing my novel. Thank you, Éilis, for encouraging me to delve into the archives of my imagination and for sharing your knowledge of folklore with me.

Deepest thanks to the Wexford Literary Festival committee: Jarlath Glynn, Carmel Harrington, Cat Hogan, Maria Nolan, Richie Cotter, Cathy Keane, Alison Martin and Paul O'Reilly. It is wonderful working for a literary festival with such an enthusiastic and energetic group of people. I am grateful for the opportunities the festival has given to me, and thoroughly enjoyed overseeing the committee for the inaugural Colm Tóibín International Short Story Award.

A very special thank-you to the incredible authors who have endorsed my work: Eoin Colfer, Éilish Ní Dhuibhne, E.R. Murray and Abi Elphinstone. Thank you all so much. Receiving endorsements for my book from such exceptionally talented authors is incredible. I cannot thank you all enough.

To the writing community in Ireland, thank you. I have met so many wonderful writers on my journey to publication. In particular I would like to thank Louise Phillips, Peter Murphy, Mary McCauley, the Gorey Writers Group and my fellow graduates from the MA in Creative Writing course whose careful critique of my work was invaluable.

And to my family:

Thank you to my parents, Séamus and Kathleen Doyle, for your constant love and encouragement. I am incredibly blessed to have you in my life. Thank you for filling my shelves with wonderful books, and for taking me to the library and reading to me long before I could talk. I am delighted that I was an only child and had you all to myself. I owe everything to you and love you both with all my heart.

To John – You are my husband and best friend. Thank you for your unconditional love and support and for giving me great advice. You are an inspiration to me.

To my three magnificent children:

Fiachra – I have never known a child to adore reading and writing as much as you do. I really enjoy our conversations about books. You are a wonderful writer and I am so very proud of you.

Caoimhe – You bake the most amazing cakes that I have ever tasted. Thank you for all the cookies that you baked for me when I was writing my book. You are such a clever, talented girl and most of all you are very kind and caring and I am lucky to have you as my daughter.

Tiernan – You are such an imaginative little boy, full of energy and joy. You also have fantastic dance moves and are the proud owner of the world's biggest smile. I have no doubt that you are destined for greatness.

Sincere thanks to my father-in-law John for the beautiful photographs, and to Mary who loved to read. We miss you more than words can say.

To all my family in England and Ireland, thank you for always being there for me. And to my friends old and new. I am blessed to have you all in my life.

Last but not least, I would like to thank the readers for picking up my book and reading it. A book only comes to life when it is read. I hope you have as much enjoyment reading *The Ghosts of Magnificent Children* as I did writing it!

Dedication

I would like to dedicate this book to my family.

To my parents Séamus and Kathleen, my husband
John and my children Fiachra, Caoimhe and Tiernan.

The Little Boy Lost

The night was dark, no father was there;
The child was wet with dew;
The mire was deep, & the child did weep,
And away the vapour flew.

William Blake – *Songs of Innocence* – **1789**

Prologue

The Girl with the Bird Living Inside

Ginny Potter is alone in a graveyard. The wind whistles through the crooked trees. Raindrops fall from silver leaves and puddles emerge like shimmering mirrors on the ground.

The blood-red moon illuminates the empty grave, where Ginny has slept for one hundred years. There are finger-marks in the soil from where she clawed her way out. Her sky-blue dress is stained with mud and torn at the sleeve. A beetle crawls across her shoulder and dirt sits beneath her fingernails.

Ivy trails along a stone wall. An owl with piercing eyes sits on a heart-shaped gate. His sharp talons glisten in the moonlight. His head swivels and his yellow eyes follow her every move.

Ginny tugs at her dress. Her lips are dry and cracked.

She looks at her headstone.

Here lies
Genevieve Potter
Born 1835
Died 1848
Age 13 years

A tear trickles down her cheek like a falling star and lands in the empty grave. A bird is singing a sad song. Ginny looks over at the owl but he is silent. She wonders where the sound is coming from. Her heart flutters and she feels tiny wings beating against her chest. There is a bird inside her ribcage.

She falls to her knees. Her ribs ache and her throat burns. She coughs and splutters. A blue-and-yellow bird flies out of her mouth. A feather drifts through the air. The bird settles on the ground and drags a worm out from under a stone.

Ginny walks around the graveyard, a pain searing through her head. She tries to remember what her life was like. In her mind, she sees a magical circus and sparkling lights. A two-headed lady from Siam with ruby-red lips, wearing a green silk kimono. A tiger pacing back and forth inside a golden cage. A woman wearing a ballet tutu and a bodice covered in pearls walking across a tightrope. And a boy with an apple-shaped birthmark on his cheek who can look into your eyes and see how you are going to die.

A sound startles Ginny. The rustling of leaves and the snap of a branch. She looks up and notices a fox with green eyes and a bushy red tail. Its ears are pricked and it looks as though it is waiting for her.

Ginny follows the fox out through the heart-shaped gates. They pass the owl with the yellow eyes who hoots in the darkness.

They walk down the mountainside towards the unsuspecting islanders who are sleeping silently in their beds. They are unaware that the Magnificent Ghost of Genevieve Potter is amongst them and things will never be the same again.

PART ONE

1848

Chapter one

London
Archibald and Mildred Luxbridge
Born 1836 and died 1848

Archie and Millie Luxbridge were no ordinary children. They were born in 1836 and belonged to one of the wealthiest families in England. Their mother Lady May Luxbridge was related to the Queen of England. There were great celebrations on the day that the twins were born. Trumpets sounded, banners were raised, and street parties took place.

For the first eleven years of their lives, the children led a charmed existence. They lived in a stately home on the outskirts of London. Their parents held lavish banquets and parties and the children were left to their own devices most of the time. They enjoyed playing hide and seek in the ancient corridors. The paintings of their ancestors, old women wearing elaborate wigs and gentlemen in riding boots with long noses, glared down on them from great heights.

On summer days, they could be found chasing peacocks with purple and red feathers through the evergreen maze which ran alongside the crystal-clear waters of the never-ending lake. Armless statues of Greek gods smiled at them from stone platforms.

Archie and Millie's clothes were cut from the finest silk which had been imported from Paris in France. And they had servants and cooks to see to their every need and to prepare the best food that money could buy.

Archie was two minutes older than his sister, and he took great care of her. At night-time, he would sneak into her bedroom and read the tales of the Brothers Grimm to her by candlelight. They would be transported to faraway lands with wicked stepmothers and evil monsters. Mildred's favourite story was "Hansel and Gretel". On rainy days, the children would dress up in costumes and re-enact the story in the great hall. They would perform beneath the silver chandelier, much to the delight of the servants.

Being the youngest child, Mildred was more demanding than her brother. She threw temper tantrums if she didn't get her own way, which meant that Archie constantly gave in to her demands. But he did not mind – in fact, Archie wanted to please his sister.

Then, on the eve of the children's twelfth birthday, something terrible happened that changed the course of their lives forever.

It started off as an ordinary day.

Archie was the first to wake and he raced into his sister's bedroom to tell her the news.

"Wake up, Millie, wake up!"

"Go away, Archie, it's too early."

From outside in the corridor Millie's pet dog Meg saw that the child's bedroom door was open, so she came in, scampered across the floor, jumped onto Millie's bed and licked her face.

"Not you as well, Meg!"

The dog was a small fluffy creature with a high-pitched bark. It ran around in circles on Millie's bed until she sat up.

"What is it, Archie? Hurry up and tell me so I can go back to sleep."

"The circus is in town!"

Millie's eyes lit up because she had always wanted to go the circus. She could hardly contain her excitement as images flashed through her mind, like pictures in a book. She imagined camels from the Nile, beautiful women balancing on the backs of grey elephants, acrobats flying through the air and tightrope walkers balancing on ropes high above her head.

"Oh, Archie, that's wonderful! But Mother would never let us go."

"But, Millie, Mother isn't here. She has gone to the country and isn't due back until tomorrow."

Just then an overweight woman wearing a black

dress and a white apron walked into the room. Two small pearl buttons strained to hold the fabric of her dress together. She had a flushed complexion, a high forehead and narrow lips. Her frizzy red hair was tied up in a bun on top of her head. She placed a silver breakfast tray on the antique writing desk in front of the window and opened the red-velvet curtains. Sunlight entered the room and illuminated dust motes that floated through the air. A brown rocking horse sat in the corner of the room beside a doll's house, which was a replica of their own home in every detail, right down to the dinnerware on the table, paintings on the walls and silver chandeliers. However, Millie's favourite object was a small white dog that resembled Meg.

The contents of the tray on the desk caused Archie's stomach to rumble. There were two bowls of porridge, a small gold side plate with sliced apple on it and a large white jug with a gold rim containing squeezed orange juice.

"Whatever are you two scheming about?" the woman asked in a strong London accent.

Millie slipped a slice of apple onto Meg's tongue, and she ate it greedily.

The woman walked over to Millie's wardrobe and took out a frilly yellow dress with a large pink bow around the centre.

"This will never do," she muttered to herself as she attempted to smooth the creases out of the dress with her left hand. "I shall have to press it myself." Then she plodded out of the room with the dress still in her hand and shut the door behind her.

The children giggled, and the dog barked.

Mildred read Archie's mind. "No, Archie, we can't."

The Luxbridge twins were born with the gift of being able to thought-read each other, which meant that they could each tell what the other one was thinking, without saying a word.

"All right, smarty pants, what was I thinking?" said Archie.

"You thought that we should sneak out tonight and go to the circus."

"You're right as usual – but why can't we?"

"Archie, it's not safe for us to be going around the streets of London on our own at night."

"Yes, but think of how much fun we could have at the circus – and we'll be back home and in our beds before anyone even knows that we're gone."

"I don't know, Archie. What will happen if I shape-shift and someone sees me?"

Ever since Millie was a baby, she had been able to shape-shift into a fox. The first time it happened was on her first birthday. Her nursemaid had gone to fetch her for her birthday party and found a fox cub sitting in her crib. The woman was panic-stricken as she thought that Millie had been eaten by the fox. She ran out of the room and down the stairs to fetch Millie's father who was reading in the library.

"Come quick, sir, it's young Millie! A fox has gobbled her up!"

Mildred's father dropped his book onto the floor and ran upstairs and into the nursery, only to find Millie giggling in her crib. The woman was dismissed immediately for causing Lord Luxbridge such distress and told never to set foot in the house again.

It didn't happen again until Millie was six years old and had gone to visit her Aunt Mary in Yorkshire. She was picking apples with Archie when she disappeared behind a tree. Archie was wondering where she had gone when moments later a small fox appeared. Archie knew straight away that the fox was his sister, as the green-velvet ribbon that she'd had in her hair was tied in a bow around the fox's neck.

Millie's parents had never witnessed her shape-shifting and she didn't want anyone to know about it. She was worried that she would be taken away and would never see her family again.

"It's all right, Millie. I'll take care of you – there's no need to worry."

Millie thought about it for a while, and eventually she decided that Archie was right: she would love to go to the circus. And for the first time in her life she would be going on a real adventure like the characters in the fairy tales that she loved to read.

Later that evening, when the servants were downstairs

having their supper, Archie and Millie crept from their rooms. They met at the top of the old spiral staircase that led to the back of the house.

As Archie looked down the winding stairs, he remembered hearing the story of a servant girl who fell to her death there many years ago. His mother had reassured him that it was nonsense and he had never told Millie about it, but he couldn't help feeling scared whenever he walked down these stairs.

Millie had secured her hair at the side of her head with a small black bow, and she wore a black dress with a white pinafore, beneath her green coat. On her feet she wore red leather boots. Archie decided to wear his hunting clothes which consisted of a bright-red riding coat with tails at the back and shiny gold buttons down the front, white breeches and his best black-leather riding boots. On his head sat a black velvet riding hat – the brim was turned upwards all round and a black satin ribbon was secured into place by a blue rosette.

"Archie, whatever do you look like?"

"It's a special occasion, Millie. I wanted to be suitably dressed."

"You'll be mistaken for the ringmaster, Archie." A shiver of excitement danced up Millie's spine.

"Come on, let's go."

They crept down the winding staircase, being careful not to make too much noise as the servants' quarters were directly beneath them. Millie could hear the servants laughing and joking and the stable boy singing a song.

Once outside, Archie checked that the coast was clear. Then they ran across the yard, past the evergreen maze and the armless statues, and alongside the never-ending lake which looked as though it were made of glass.

Two white swans swam past and they turned their yellow beaks away in disgust – it was as if they knew where the children were going.

Once the children had reached the gates they walked into a narrow lane, and Millie started to cry.

"Let's go back, Archie, I'm scared."

"It's all right, Millie. Look!"

Archie took off his hat. Beneath it was a blue satin bag tied with ribbon. He opened the ribbon and showed the contents of the bag to Millie who gasped in amazement.

"Breadcrumbs! What in the world are they for?"

"I brought them in case we get lost. Here, help me to scatter them."

Millie opened her hand and Archie poured some breadcrumbs into it.

"You really do think of everything, Archie Luxbridge!"

The children walked on, leaving a trail of breadcrumbs behind them. The further they walked from their home, the closer they got to the horror that awaited them.

"We're nearly there, Millie."

Archie had visited the city many times before with his father and thought he knew his way around. However, Millie wasn't at all confident. It was her first time to be out in public unchaperoned. She knew that it was highly inappropriate for a young lady of her social standing to be wandering around the streets of London at night. She imagined her mother's disgust and outrage if she ever found out. She moved closer to Archie as they walked along the cobbled streets.

Music spilled out of the windows of a tavern called the Wild Boar. Millie looked through the window and saw a young woman in a frilly orange dress standing beside a piano, singing a song. Another woman in a black-lace corseted dress sat on the knee of a bald man. She poured him a drink and wiped the sweat from his head with a grubby grey handkerchief.

"Come on, Millie," said Archie.

A girl Millie's age sat begging in front of a toyshop. The shop was still open, late though it was, and brightly lit up. Millie could see a jack-in-the-box and a doll's house in the window. She wondered why the girl did not go home. She had no shoes on her feet, and grime sat between her toes.

"Please spare me some change."

She held out two dirty hands and tugged at Millie's dress. Millie screamed.

"Leave her alone!" Archie cried.

The girl loosened her grip and coughed up green phlegm which she spat onto the cobbled street.

The smell of rotten vegetables wafted through the air, and Millie felt sick.

"Are we nearly there, Archie?"

"Look!"

Millie followed her brother's finger which pointed to the most amazing sight that she had ever seen. The circus was there in front of her. A huge tent – the Big Top – had been erected in the centre of a park and a crescent-shaped moon smiled in the sky above it.

Archie pulled his father's silver pocket watch out of his coat and, when she saw it, Millie gasped and put her hand to her mouth.

"Archie, that's Father's watch! Whatever are you doing with it?"

"I am just borrowing it, Millie, so that I can keep an eye on the time."

Archie put the watch safely back into his pocket, and they walked on towards the shimmering lights.

They could see people queuing up at a box which resembled a coffin, to buy tickets for the performance. A demure lady in a sequinned costume stood at the entrance to the circus tent collecting tickets from the people going in. Her hips swung like a pendulum as she moved back and forth, while her heels punctured the grass with tiny holes. Millie was mesmerised by her.

"Come on, Millie."

Archie dragged his sister by the hand. He was hoping that they could slip in at the back of the tent without paying. They ran past a cage, and a lion roared. Millie fell back and landed in the mud. Archie helped her up.

Then they saw a tall man dressed in black, twirling a pointy black moustache as he stood at another tent. A large crowd of people had gathered around him. A wooden sign with the words *FREAK SHOW* was pinned to the entrance of the tent and Millie wondered what a freak show was. The children listened as the man began to speak to the crowd. He was as thin as a blade of grass and as he opened his mouth he revealed a mouth full of gold teeth.

"Roll, up, roll up! What you are about to witness are some of the Seven Wonders of the World! We have a Bearded Lady from a foreign land! Tom Thumb and Thumbelina, the tiniest man and woman on the planet! The Mermaid Woman – a curious creature with the head of a monkey and the tail of a fish! The Two-Headed Woman from Siam! And, for the first time, the extraordinary Elephant Man!"

People gasped in amazement and whispered to each other.

"Yes, ladies and gentlemen, a man who is half-elephant half-human! Allow yourselves to be terrified as you experience the Freak Show!"

Millie stood in awe as she listened to the man

17

speak. She never knew that such people existed.

"Archie, can we go and . . ."

Millie looked around and realised that Archie was gone. She ran through the crowds, past acrobats and clowns. She looked everywhere, but she could not find Archie. Then she spotted her father's pocket watch in the mud – it shone in the moonlight. She bent down and tried to pick it up, but it was wet, so it slipped through her fingers and fell to the ground again.

Then someone grabbed her.

Millie screamed, but no-one could hear her above the sound of the chatter and laughter. A gloved hand moved over her mouth so that she couldn't breathe. Then she was lifted through the air. She kicked her legs and turned her head. As she looked at the man's face, she saw his pointy black moustache and, when he smiled to reveal his gold teeth, she realised that it was the ringmaster.

He dragged her away from the crowd towards the back of the Big Top. There were three cages there and the ringmaster pulled her towards the third one. Her heart thumped in her chest as she thought of the lion she'd seen earlier. Then the ringmaster opened the cage with a silver key which hung from a chain around his neck and thrust her inside. As he turned the key in the rusty lock, she noticed that it had the image of a bird engraved on it. She thought it looked like the key to a beautiful palace and she cried as she suddenly realised that she might never see her home again.

At first Millie thought that she was alone as it took a moment for her eyes to adjust to the darkness.

"Archie!" she cried, covering her face with her hands despondently.

"It is all right, my dear, don't cry."

Millie heard the muffled voice coming from the corner of the cage. Then she heard the person breathing heavily and shuffling across the cage towards her.

Millie peeped through her fingers to behold the most extraordinary sight she had ever seen. A man with the face of an elephant was peering at her through the darkness.

Chapter two

The Girl and the Circus

One week later

Heavy fog lay on the River Thames. As the moon rose in the sky, the fog burst through the bustling city streets. It swirled around the ankles of people who dared to be out on such a bitterly cold evening. The smell of rotting apples and fish meandered through the long lanes. Street sellers had their wooden carts piled high with fruit and vegetables.

A woman walked down the street. Her red petticoat was visible and matched the slip of silk she wore around her neck. She paused at a flower stall to pick out a bunch of yellow roses which matched her dress. She paid the old woman behind the stall and continued down the lane. Her heels clicked as she walked. The smell of expensive perfume lingered in the air after her.

A boy with a red face stood still on the lamplit

street. He had a streak of dirt on his cheek and his lips were chapped from the cold. A tall gentleman strolled by, wearing a top hat which made him look even taller. A copy of the *Illustrated London News* was under his arm and he stopped briefly beneath the gas-lamp to read about the ongoing cholera epidemic. The red-faced boy coughed and the gentleman pulled a handkerchief from the breast pocket of his tailcoat, covered his mouth with it and hurried away.

The chorus of street sellers began to shout as the man hurried past.

"Come and get your apples!"

"Roses for sale!"

"Fresh fish caught today!"

Theo stood at one end of Dreary Lane and Ginny waited at the other. She hunkered down like a cat waiting to pounce. They had been watching the young woman for over a week now. Every evening she took the same route home. Judging from all her frills and flounces, the children presumed she was coming from a dancehall.

As she came to the end of the lane, Ginny coughed, drawing her attention.

"Please, missus, spare us some change!" She held out a dirty hand.

The woman looked down at Ginny, who wore a shabby grey dress without a coat despite the cold. Ginny's porcelain skin was white as snow. Her long, blonde hair shimmered under the moonlight. Her blue eyes shone like whirlpools. The woman had never seen such a pretty girl before. She wondered where Ginny's mother was. If she were her daughter she would have taken better care of her.

The woman opened the silver clasp on her purse and handed Ginny a shiny gold coin. Then she watched as Ginny's blue eyes sparkled and her cheeks glowed.

"You shouldn't be out here."

"Thanks, missus."

"Go on, get yourself some food and go home."

Ginny glanced back along the lane. Theo should have been here by now. Ginny didn't think she could stall her for much longer. But, as she looked into the woman's eyes, she realised they shouldn't rob her. Perhaps this was her mother who had abandoned her at the gates of the orphanage all those years ago.

"Can I come home with you?"

"I'm sorry?"

"I need your help."

"I really must go."

As the woman turned to leave, Ginny jumped to her feet and grabbed her by the arm.

"Wait!" she said.

"I'll call the police if you don't let me go."

"I want to show you something – please wait!"

Ginny started to cough and cough. The woman thought she was choking and was about to go and get help when, all of a sudden, a bright blue feather flew out of Ginny's mouth and landed at the woman's feet. Ginny continued coughing, then opened her mouth wide and a blue-and-yellow bird flew out. It perched on the woman's shoulder, spread its wings and sang the most beautiful song the woman had ever heard.

"How did you d-do that . . . I mean . . . You're a special girl, aren't you?"

The bird flew between Ginny and the woman as they spoke.

"When I was born, I was unable to breathe so the doctors examined me. That's when they discovered that I have a birdcage instead of a ribcage. Blue lives inside me."

"Well, I never!" The woman held out her middle finger and the bird perched on it.

Ginny looked down the road again. The woman followed her gaze.

"Are you waiting for someone?"

"Yes, my friend Theo. He should be here by now."

"Why don't you and Blue come home with me?"

"I was wrong to ask you. I can't."

"Of course you can. It will be warmer at my place than it is out here."

"I can't."

"I might even have some food for Blue there. What do you think?"

Ginny looked at Blue as he flew through the air. H

instincts told her that she should protect her feathered friend so she opened her mouth and he flew back inside. He glided down her throat and into the safety of his birdcage. Then he sat on the perch made from Ginny's bone, placed his head under his wing and fell asleep.

There was no sign of Theo. It was possible he had met up with the Foster Gang, a group of petty thieves that he often spent time with. Ginny did not like them so she decided to take the woman up on her offer and together they walked down the moonlit street.

Theo watched Ginny and the woman walk down Dreary Lane. He felt protective of his beautiful friend and the strange little bird that lived inside her.

They had first met a year earlier when Theo was walking down Bleeding Heart Street one night, after he had spent the evening pickpocketing with the Foster Gang. He was laughing to himself and jingling the coins in his pocket. It had started to snow earlier in the day and the snow was at least a foot deep by the time he made his way home. He fastened his long black overcoat over his waistcoat and shirt, and it was then that he heard a girl screaming. At first he thought it was a cat and paid no attention to it, but then he saw a trail of red blood in the snow which led him to Ginny. She had been robbed and left for dead. He had taken care of her since that night and now he thought of her as his family. At first Ginny was scared of him and Theo didn't blame her as he had his head shaved and there was an unusual apple-shaped birthmark on his cheek. But after a while she began to trust him and let him look after her.

The sound of the woman's footsteps reminded Theo of a ticking clock. He watched her and Ginny until they became no more than a silhouette. When they were a safe distance away he decided to follow them. The fog blanketed the sky and whispered its secrets to the stars. There was something haunting and gloomy about the night. The lane was dark and quiet and Theo had the unnerving feeling that he was being watched. He had just decided to go back the way he came when a man stepped out of the shadows and into his path.

An ice-cold shiver ran up Theo's spine.

"Watch it, mister!" He went to walk left, then right, but each time the man blocked his path. "What are you playing at?"

The man stood in front of Theo. He wore a long black cloak and a top hat sat squarely on his head. He opened his cloak just enough for Theo to make out the outline of a knife hanging on his belt. The man reached into an inside pocket and took out a cigar and some matches. He lit the cigar.

Theo coughed as the man blew smoke rings into the air.

"I don't want any trouble, mister."

"I'm sure you don't."

"Let me pass."

Theo tried to push by but the man didn't move. Theo knew he could use his ability but, if he did, he would only draw attention to himself. He was already in trouble with the law.

The man dropped the cigar and grabbed Theo by the wrist. He pulled the knife out from under his cape and prodded it into Theo's side.

"Listen here, wicked boy. Do as I say and you won't get hurt."

There was nothing Theo could do. If he called for help who would listen to him? He was a thief and a beggar. The man forced Theo to walk down by the river and towards a circus that emerged like a nightmare out of the fog.

The man moved the knife to Theo's back and pressed it against his spine.

An old woman selling oysters screeched with laughter and opened her mouth, revealing a toothless grin.

Two men were huddled around a newspaper and one of them shouted into the night sky. *"Cholera epidemic claims another life!"*

Two grey rats ran between the legs of a woman in a purple dress who smelt of gin. She had a shock of black hair piled on top of her head and a wart on the end of her nose. Theo watched the rats scurry behind the wooden carts and onto the banks of the Thames. He watched them until they vanished into the mist.

The knife cut through Theo's shirt and pierced his skin.

"Watch it, mister!" he said.

A dog barked somewhere in the distance and the waning moon peered down from the black sky.

They stopped outside the Black Swan Inn. Theo had been there before with some of the Foster Gang. He knew it was a popular place with smugglers and thieves. A young boy stood in the doorway and played a merry tune on an accordion as two men brawled outside. The man winning the fight was about six feet tall. The sleeves of his red-plaid shirt were rolled up to reveal the tattoo of a woman on his wrinkled arm. His opponent was a dark skinny man with a hump on his back and a wooden leg. The man in the red shirt delivered the final blow. Theo watched as the skinny man's front tooth flew through the air like a snowflake.

Silence greeted them as they walked into the inn. Theo could feel the blade of the knife against his back. The man in the cape was the first to speak.

"Good evening, gentlemen."

The man grasped Theo's arm and marched him over to the bar. He did not loosen his grip on him as he ordered a glass of gin from a red-haired barmaid. She wore a patch over her right eye and scanned the room with her left. She did not seem to notice the worrying predicament that Theo had found himself in – or, if she did, she did not offer him any assistance.

He drank the gin and slammed the empty glass on the bar.

"Let's go."

"Where?" cried Theo.

"Shut up and keep walking."

Outside the inn there was no sign of the crowd that was there earlier.

The cold air wrestled with the man's black cloak and a gust of wind caused it to rise like the wings of a bat. Theo had the distinct feeling that they were being watched. He heard the sound of footsteps approaching and a rush of adrenaline surged through his veins. Maybe this was his chance to escape. Maybe the Foster gang were looking for him!

But it was only one man. He came to a halt in front of Theo who screamed with fright. Before him stood a man whose entire face was covered in coarse hair. He was wearing a brown suit, with a white shirt beneath it and had a flat cap on his head.

The man who held Theo grew fierce with rage. "Shut your mouth, boy, or this knife will become very well acquainted with your heart."

Theo did as he was told.

"Here, take the knife and don't take any nonsense, do you hear?" the man in the cloak said.

The man with the hairy face nodded and grabbed

Theo. He pressed the knife against his side and pushed him forward.

They walked along the dark, empty street. The only sound that could be heard was the sound of their footsteps and a cat screeching somewhere in the distance.

Ginny walked along the riverbank. The woman's skirt rustled in the breeze and the smell of stagnant water filled the air. Ginny noticed a scruffy black dog scratching its flea-ridden body. They passed a dilapidated row of houses. A woman with a head of black curls opened a window on the top floor of one of the houses and shouted at a man in the street. The man looked up at her, his face red, his nose large and pockmarked.

"Watch out!" shouted the woman. She flung a bucket of urine from the open window, narrowly missing Ginny. It covered the red-faced man from head to toe.

"That should sober you up!" the woman shouted before slamming the window shut.

Somewhere in the distance Ginny heard a baby cry.

"Here we are, dear."

They had stopped outside a boarding house. A timber sign advertised rooms to let. The woman opened the door. The smell of stew hovered in the air and Ginny's stomach growled.

On the first floor, Ginny looked through a crack in a door into a small room. An old Chinese man with hair sprouting out of his ears was sitting on a small kitchen chair, a bowl of steaming food on the table in front of him. A young woman with tired eyes and shiny black hair was in the background, holding a child in her arms.

Ginny followed the woman until they arrived at the top floor. The door that led to the woman's room had a small piece of paper stuck to it which said:

Notice to Evict

The woman flicked a nervous smile at Ginny, then pulled the note off the door, crumpled it up into a ball and stuck it into the pocket of her dress.

The room was bigger than Ginny had expected. The sound of street sellers could be heard from the open window. The woman went over and shut it. There was a large metal-framed bed in the centre of the room. Dresses and petticoats were flung on top of it. Beneath the bed was a row of women's shoes. The woman kicked off the yellow-and-black pair she was wearing and put them carefully between a green pair with a low heel and a red pair that had scuffed pointy toes.

In the corner of the room was a French dressing-screen with two birds of paradise painted on the front. The woman walked behind it and began to undress.

"Don't mind me."

Ginny sat on the edge of the bed which cried out as she sat down.

Ginny looked at the screen. If she squinted her eyes, she could make out the silhouette of the woman's slim body as she undressed. Ginny felt embarrassed and looked away. She noticed three glass jars containing unusual objects. They were on a shelf next to a wardrobe with gold handles. Ginny stood up and walked over to the jars, which were filled with liquid. The first jar contained a duckling with two heads. Ginny stared at the small bird floating in the liquid. Its eyeballs were missing and the feathers had been plucked from its frail body. The second jar was much larger in size, and secured with a brown lid. It contained a deformed goldfish with a black beak. Ginny picked up the jar to examine the fish more closely. It was heavier than she had expected and she almost dropped it. The fish had tiny fingers, instead of fins, which stretched out from its golden body. Floating beside the fish was a lizard with two tongues. Ginny had never seen such oddities before, although she had heard that they were popular in circus freak shows. The third jar contained what Ginny believed to be an animal's brain, although it could also have belonged to a small child.

Ginny stepped back from the shelf as she realised that she didn't know anything about the woman she'd met in the street. She began to wonder if she was in danger.

"Why do you have these jars?"

Ginny wanted to inspect the preserved animals further, but there was something about them that scared her and she suddenly felt as if she couldn't breathe. She walked across the room and opened the window – the latch was stiff and she had to use all her strength to open it. A horse and carriage passed beneath the window and she imagined the woman sitting in the carriage with her colourful petticoats, a blend of greens and yellow swaying in the breeze. Ginny thought she would make a beautiful sight.

"Don't you like them?"

The woman appeared at Ginny's left shoulder. She was dressed in a pink ballet tutu which was covered in flounces and frills. Her bodice was embroidered with pearls and tightly laced with a blue ribbon. Pale cream stockings adorned her slender legs and on her small feet were ballerina slippers. A mother-of-pearl hairclip secured her red hair in a loose chignon at the nape of her neck. She held a Japanese fan. With one flick of the wrist the fan came to life, revealing the image of a geisha. The woman peered over it at Ginny.

"Like what?"

"My collection of jars, of course."

The woman bent her body backwards so that her head reached the floor. She touched the ground with her fingers. Ginny thought that she resembled a crab.

"No, not really," Ginny said.

"What's your name, cherub?"

"Ginny."

"Allow me to introduce myself, Ginny. My name is Antonia Rivenio the Great."

Ginny thought that the woman *was* great, as she flipped her body back into an upright position.

"Tell me, where is your family?"

As Antonia spoke, she did the splits. Then she sat in the centre of the floor with her legs crossed and her arms outstretched.

"I don't have a family."

"How strange!"

"They abandoned me at the gates of an orphanage when they found out I was different."

"How sad."

Antonia stood up.

"I don't blame them," Ginny said, smiling at Antonia.

"Well, you should join my family then. You would fit right in."

"I-I couldn't."

"Nonsense!"

"But what about Theo?"

"Who-O?"

"Theo, my friend."

"Oh, the boy. The one you were supposed to meet. Listen, Ginny, I can tell you a thing or two about boys."

"Theo is my friend."

Ginny blushed. She was defending Theo. The same Theo who drove her mad, the same Theo with whom she argued all day long. But he was her family.

"He isn't much of a friend if he left you down a dark lane on your own."

Ginny bit her bottom lip. She could feel Blue fluttering around inside her chest as he always did when she felt sad. Somehow the small blue bird knew exactly how Ginny felt.

"Tell you what – let's dress you up and I can take you to meet my family."

"Where do they live?"

"You'll see. Now let's have a look at you."

Antonia opened the wardrobe and a mountain of clothes tumbled onto the floor. Inside the door was a long mirror with a crack in it. Antonia rummaged through the pile of clothes and flung them up into the air. Some of them narrowly missed the small black stove that stood in the corner of the room.

Ginny coughed and Blue appeared. The small bird fluttered its wings, then flew around the room dodging the brightly coloured fabrics as Antonia threw them around the room.

"Here we are!"

Antonia stood up, holding a sky-blue dress. It had flowers delicately embroidered around the neckline and a small gold rope around the waist.

"Perfect. Go on then – try it on!"

Ginny stepped in behind the dressing screen. Blue looked down at the birds of paradise while she undressed and slipped the dress over her head. The delicate fabric brushed against her skin. Ginny had never worn such a beautiful dress before.

Antonia gasped as Ginny stepped out from behind the screen and Blue sang a bright little tune.

"Sit down. I'll try and do something with that hair of yours."

Antonia went over to a wooden shelf beside her bed. It was crooked and looked as though it would topple over at any moment. On top of it were two books: *A Christmas Carol* by Charles Dickens and a copy of the Bible with a worn leather cover. They stood side by side like soldiers going into battle. Next to the Bible was a silver hairbrush. It had bright red strands of hair woven between the bristles.

Antonia took the brush over to Ginny, who had sat down on a three-legged stool by the stove. The sound of a flute on the street below entered the room, then a woman's scream. Blue flew over to the window and pecked at the glass. Ginny closed her eyes and thought of Theo. Antonia pulled the red hairs out of the brush, untied Ginny's blue ribbon and brushed her crinkled hair until it shone. When she was finished, she led Ginny across the room so that she could see her reflection in the mirror.

"A few finishing touches and you'll be ready."

Antonia slipped a pair of green shoes onto Ginny's feet. They were a perfect fit. Then she unhooked a gold cross and chain from her own neck and placed it around Ginny's. A few moments later she got down on her knees, stretched her right arm under the bed and produced a crown made from beautiful silk flowers which matched the shoes perfectly. She stood up and placed it on Ginny's head.

Then she clapped her hands together and cartwheeled across the room.

Back on her feet again, she raised a finger and said, "But wait! We can't have you going out on a cold night like this without a shawl, my cherub." She disappeared behind the dressing screen and reappeared moments later resembling a beautiful blue sky on a summer's day. The reason for this optical illusion was the blue shawl that she wore: it had small white clouds embroidered on it, the edges of the clouds stitched with a fine silver thread.

She took off the shawl and handed it to Ginny.

"Here you go, my lovely. Just remember: every cloud has a silver lining."

Ginny struggled to hold back the tears of joy which stung her eyes. She had never been treated so kindly by anyone before and felt as though she were in the middle of a wonderful dream.

Blue flew around the room and landed on the dusty-pink shade of a lamp on a chest of drawers.

"I almost forgot."

Antonia walked over to the wooden chest of drawers.

"Thanks for reminding me, Blue," she said.

The birds-of-paradise pattern was etched into two panels at the front of the drawers. There was a keyhole.

Antonia put her hand down the front of her laced bodice and pulled out a small golden key which had a small bird engraved on it. She used it to open the drawer.

"This is my secret hiding place, Ginny, so don't tell anyone, will you?"

Ginny shook her head and smiled as Blue flew over to a painting on the wall and sat on its frame. The picture showed a ship in the middle of a storm. Ginny moved closer to Antonia and peered into the drawer where she noticed a crocheted white shawl which had Antonia's name woven into it in gold thread.

"Like it, do you?"

Ginny blushed to be caught staring and looked away.

"It's all right – have a closer look."

Antonia handed Ginny the shawl and she traced the delicate name with her finger.

"My mother made it for my christening."

"It's beautiful. Where is she now?"

Antonia had a faraway look in her eyes. A red curl came loose from her hairclip and fell over her left ear. She took the shawl from Ginny and held it close to her face.

"My parents were killed in a fire when I was a baby. I was taken in by the circus."

"I'm sorry."

"It was a long time ago now. I still have a few things to remember them by."

Antonia reached into the drawer again and took out a small music box with a silver handle. On top of it was a ballerina. Antonia turned the handle and the ballerina started to dance. Ginny hadn't heard the music before. Antonia told her it was from an opera by Mozart called *The Magic Flute*. Blue fluttered his wings and danced in the air.

When the music stopped Antonia placed the music box back into the drawer and covered it with the shawl. She then took out a gold bottle of perfume.

"Here it is! Mr Zachariah Badblood gave this to me – he brought it back from Paris. He said that all the women there are wearing it."

Suddenly Ginny remembered Theo.

"Antonia, I have to go."

"You can't go out on your own at this time of night."

"I have to meet Theo – he'll be looking for me."

"Why don't you wait until morning? It will be easier to find him in the daylight."

Before Ginny had time to answer, there was a knock on the door. Ginny opened her mouth wide and Blue flew down into her ribcage.

Antonia answered the door and a man with a long, black beard and dark eyes entered the room. His profile looked like a crescent moon. He was the thinnest man that Ginny had ever seen. He was holding a violin in his left hand and a bow in his right. He placed the instrument under his chin and started to play a sad tune. After him came a man playing a flute. He wore a purple-velvet overcoat and had a red flower pinned to his left lapel. On his head was a grey hat.

Antonia was about to shut the door when two identical women appeared. They had porcelain skin, red lips and shiny black hair. Ginny was astonished when she realised that they had only one body between them, adorned with a blue silk kimono. On the front of the kimono was the image of a Japanese garden. Beneath the kimono were two dainty feet. Ginny opened her mouth to speak but she didn't know which of the women's heads to direct her questions to. She rubbed her eyes, then counted again: two arms, two legs, one body and two heads. Ginny had never encountered Siamese Twins before. She looked over at Antonia to gauge her reaction. However, she was deep in conversation with a tiny woman no bigger than a child. Blue sensed something was wrong and flew out of Ginny's ribcage to have a look.

"Well, well, what have we here?"

A man stood in the doorway. He wore a black cloak and twirled a pointy moustache between his fingers.

Antonia ran to Ginny and took her by the hand.

"Mr Zachariah Badblood, I would like to introduce you to Ginny."

"Ginny, the Bird Girl, how nice to finally make your acquaintance." Badblood took hold of Ginny's hand and kissed it.

39

"There must be some mistake," Ginny said as she pulled back her hand.

Ginny looked around for Antonia, but couldn't see her anywhere.

"I don't make mistakes, girl."

"The Bird Girl is not familiar with how things work yet," giggled one of the Siamese Twins.

"Mr Moonshine, some music, please." Badblood clicked his fingers and the fiddler played a lively tune.

Antonia appeared from behind the dressing screen. She was now wearing a man's tuxedo. Her red hair was slicked back into a pigtail and a fake moustache clung to her upper lip. In her hands, she had two glasses of red wine. She walked over to the Siamese Twins who were looking at Ginny suspiciously and handed them the drinks. When she caught Ginny's eye, she saluted her.

Badblood clicked his fingers again and the music stopped. Ginny heard the sound of footsteps coming up the stairs and then Theo's voice.

"Let me go!"

Ginny ran towards the still-open door.

Theo was struggling as a man whose entire face was covered in coarse black hair held onto him. He had a knife made from bone pressed against Theo's back. Ginny could see that Theo's shirt was torn and a spot of blood glistened on the knife.

The man pushed Theo towards Ginny and placed

the knife down on Antonia's dressing table.

"Oh, how nice!" Badblood said. "Together at last! Mr Moonshine, some music, please!"

The fiddler began to play again.

"Are you all right, Theo?"

Theo put his arms around her protectively. "Yes, I'm fine, Ginny."

"But you're bleeding!"

"It's nothing." Then he whispered, "Who are these people?"

"They're from a circus. I'm scared, Theo."

"We'll think of something."

Antonia walked over to Ginny and Theo.

"How could you do this?" said Ginny. "You tricked me!"

"And were you and your little friend here not going to trick me earlier?"

"What do you mean?"

"Out on the street – you were going to rob me."

"But I didn't!"

"I mean you no harm, Ginny. I am saving you from a life of crime."

"She doesn't need saving!"

Theo stood in front of Ginny. Antonia pushed him to one side and took hold of Ginny's hand.

"Look at the clothes I've given you. I can promise you a better life now. Mr Zachariah has always done right by me. I never wanted for anything."

Ginny looked at Theo. Maybe Antonia was right. All she had known since she met Theo was a life of crime. Perhaps the circus would offer her a better way of life, an honest way, and Antonia had been good to her so far. She began to smile.

"There's the girl."

Theo looked around the room. His eyes fell upon the knife on the dressing table. He moved towards it as stealthily as a cat stalking a bird and, when he was sure that no-one was looking, he picked up the knife and slipped it into the pocket of his coat. Theo did not trust these people and he knew he would do everything he could to escape.

Chapter three

Badblood's Circus

Ginny was captivated by Badblood's Circus. The red-and-white-striped dome reminded her of candy canes. It was held up by thick frayed ropes, which were secured into the yellow grass by large wooden pegs. A magpie pecked at the rope. His sharp black beak pulled at threads as though they were worms. Ginny imagined what would happen if the tent collapsed. The wind blew the leaves from the trees and scattered them around the field. The bare branches swayed in the breeze while the red-and-brown leaves crunched underfoot.

A crowd of people had gathered at a small wooden box. It was a coffin, standing upright, and there was a hatch in the front of it. The Siamese Twins stood behind the hatch, dressed in a green silk floral kimono.

White powder covered their faces, and their bow-shaped lips were drawn on with dark-red lipstick. Their shiny black hair was adorned with blue flowers and cascaded in waves over their shoulders. Their beauty transfixed Ginny. The excited crowd was captivated by them. The word *TICKETS* was painted in oxblood on a piece of jagged timber, which had been secured to the front of the box with four rusty nails.

A blonde girl in a frilly pink dress stood beside a large man in a brown overcoat. She was licking an ice cream. The ice cream had begun to melt, and a white stain in the shape of a fox had formed on the girl's dress. In between licks, she smiled at Ginny to reveal a gap where her two front teeth should have been.

An old woman, wrapped in a black shawl, walked through the crowd. Her head was bent, and there was a hump on her back. Her long fingers were covered in green warts and dirt sat beneath her fingernails. Long, grey hair was plaited down her back, and her chin was covered in coarse silver hair. A crooked nose protruded from her moon-shaped face.

The man in the brown coat moved forward, but the girl remained in the same spot licking her ice cream until the crowd swallowed her up.

Ginny watched the old woman speak to the little girl although she could not hear what they were saying. Then the woman took the child by the hand and led her away through the crowd. The man turned around to look for the child, but she was gone. Ginny watched as panic and fear distorted his features. He pushed his way back through the people with his elbows.

"Time to go, Ginny," Antonia said.

Two burly constables blowing whistles ran past them and parted the crowd. One of them was overweight and struggled to keep up with the younger one who was brandishing a truncheon.

Antonia pinched Ginny's arm and refused to let go so Ginny had to go with her. She could feel a bruise begin to form beneath her skin.

As the man in the brown coat was about to disappear, Ginny turned her head and saw the girl run into his arms. He picked her up and twirled her around in delight. Her sticky fingers were wrapped around his large neck.

Antonia loosened her grip on Ginny's arm and smiled at her, as she had done when they first met. Ginny wondered if Antonia had meant to hurt her. It certainly felt like it, although she thought that she must have been mistaken for Antonia had been so kind to her. Ginny felt a shiver dance down her spine as Antonia took her by the hand and led her away from the Big Top and the noise of the circus.

They walked past three metal cages. Four wooden wheels with large spokes elevated each of them from the ground. Ginny peered into the dark cage. At first she thought it was empty, but then a lion with a golden mane ran to the front of the cage and roared at her. Ginny screamed and fell back into Antonia's arms. Antonia sniggered at her and for the second time that evening Ginny doubted her judgement of Antonia's character.

"Don't mind Leo. He wouldn't harm you. He ain't got no teeth."

Ginny wasn't so sure as the animal swung its large claws at the bars and turned its head to one side. It was as though it was sizing her up for its next meal.

Ginny stood well back from the second cage which was much bigger than the first. Nettles and dandelions had formed around the wheels which had sunk into the mud. A ladybird walked up the stalk of a dock leaf, jumped onto the wheel, and then walked into the dark cage. Ginny saw something move at the back of the cage. It sounded like feet shuffling and a chain being dragged. Ginny covered her eyes with her hands and peered out through her fingers. A brown bear came into view and pressed its paws against the bars. Ginny had never seen such a sad-looking creature in all her life. The bear appeared to be pleading with Ginny to help him. Against her better judgement, she slipped her hand in through the bars of the cage and stroked the animal's head. Its brown fur was matted with blood, and there was a bald patch around its waist where a metal chain dug into its skin.

It began to rain hard, and instinctively the bear

moved back into the shadows. Ginny shivered as the wind blew her hair around her shoulders. She walked over to the final cage, with the memory of the bear's sad face etched beneath her eyelids.

The crescent moon had risen in the sky, and a slither of light illuminated the night. The final cage was green. Inside the cage was a little girl sleeping on a bed of hay. She had lank brown hair tied up at the side with a black bow. Her knees were tucked beneath her black dress. Ginny could see a pair of boots sticking out – they were made of soft, red leather which told Ginny that the girl came from a wealthy family. Two hands joined in prayer rested beneath a small dimpled chin. Ginny wondered what the girl was dreaming about, and where her parents were. She had the strangest feeling she had seen the child before, although she could not think where.

In the farthest corner of the cage was the strangest-looking creature that Ginny had ever come across. At first Ginny thought the moonlight was playing tricks with her mind. The creature looked so strange that Ginny pressed her face against the cage to get a closer look.

The moonlight shone on a man with the face of an elephant. Ginny gulped in shock, and Blue, sensing Ginny's fear, flapped his wings inside her ribcage. Ginny held her hand over her mouth to prevent the small bird from flying out.

"That's the Elephant Man, and the little one is Millie," Antonia whispered into Ginny's ear.

Even the girl's name sounded familiar.

The rain turned to sleet and dark clouds moved like fists over the waning moon.

"Don't dawdle, Ginny."

"Why is the girl, Millie, in a cage?"

"Come on. The circus will begin in less than an hour, and I'm not ready yet."

Before Ginny could say any more, Antonia gripped her by the hand and together they walked across the field and into a small yellow tent.

A breeze followed Antonia and Ginny into the tent, which was carpeted in worn oriental rugs. Candles flickered on a bookshelf. There was a strange smell of burning incense and it reminded Ginny of being in a church.

Theo was sitting crossed-legged on a rug while a white Jack Russell Terrier sat on his lap and licked his neck. When the dog saw Antonia, it ran over to her and yapped at her ankles. Theo took no notice of Ginny. He was angry with her, she could tell, and who could blame him? She had got them into this mess in the first place.

Badblood was there, leaning against the bookshelf, peeling the skin of an apple with a silver penknife. Ginny watched as the apple peel fell to the floor.

There were four books on a table in the centre of the

room and beside the books were two cages. The first cage contained a fluffy white rabbit; it sat on a bed of straw and chewed a piece of carrot. In the second cage were two lovebirds with green and orange feathers. They were perched on a piece of wood and sang to each other.

The old woman who had tried to abduct the girl was there too. She held a candle in a pewter candlestick. The wax dripped onto her fingers. Crow's feet clawed at the skin around her bulging eyes which looked as though they were about to pop out of their sockets and roll across the floor.

Ginny heard a child crying. At first she couldn't tell where the sound was coming from. She looked at Theo who shrugged his shoulders and looked away.

The old woman flapped her black shawl, like a matador in a bullfight. The sudden snapping noise of the shawl must have startled the crying child as a boy of about twelve years of age old ran out from behind the bookcase. He was sweating so much that his skin looked shiny, and his eyes were red from crying. Ginny noticed that his resemblance to Millie, the girl asleep in the cage, was striking. He wore a long red coat with tails, white breeches and black riding boots. On his head was a black velvet riding hat with a round brim, decorated with a blue rosette. He rubbed his eyes with the back of his hand and walked over to Ginny, who placed her hand reassuringly on his shoulder.

"It's going to be all right," she said to him.

"Enough of that," said Antonia, who was now wearing a silver dress.

Ginny wondered how she had got changed so quickly. Then she noticed a dressing screen in the corner of the tent. It was identical to the one back in the lodging house, with birds of paradise painted on the front. The clothes she had taken off were hanging over the edge of the screen. Red curls hung around her ears, and a silver crown with a yellow feather rested on her head. It was one of Blue's feathers. Her oval-shaped eyes were outlined in black. They looked bigger than usual and her eyelashes fluttered like butterfly wings when she blinked.

Badblood walked across the tent, took Antonia's hand in his and kissed it. The small dog ran around in circles chasing its tail, then stopped for a moment to sniff the black shawl on the ground and growled at Theo, while the old woman cackled in delight.

The boy stepped closer to Ginny. She could see the fear in his eyes and thought about the girl in the cage. She wondered where their parents were. She could tell from the way that the boy was looking at her that he was pleading for help and her instincts told her that he and the girl didn't belong somewhere like this.

Badblood twirled his moustache between his fingers. He picked up a wooden cane which was leaning against the bookcase, then he walked out of the tent and into the darkness with Antonia by his side.

"Don't try any funny business," said the old woman as she rapped her knuckles on the table. Purple veins ran like rivers under her paper-thin skin and she screwed up her face so tight that her eyes bulged even more. She wagged a dirty finger at the children. The dog whimpered and ran under the table.

A worn mattress lay beside the dressing screen. The old woman belched, went over to the mattress and lay on it. A plume of dust rose and put one of the candles out.

Ginny coughed as the smoke tickled her throat, and Blue tumbled out of her mouth. He flew around the room, stopping momentarily on top of the birdcage. He looked in at the lovebirds, but when they didn't pay any attention to him he flew onto the boy's shoulder instead. The boy laughed as Blue nudged his ear and tickled it with his yellow beak.

Within seconds the old woman was snoring loudly – but she kept her two eyes open and on the children at all times. Whenever they moved, her protruding eyeballs followed them. The children could hear the sound of a drum and a lion's roar and people clapping. The circus had begun.

Theo walked over to Ginny and the boy.

"We need to get out of here," he muttered. His face looked green under the candlelight.

"I know," said Ginny.

"What's your name, boy?" Theo asked.

"Archie."

Theo looked at Ginny. They both realised who the boy was.

"Are you Archibald Luxbridge?" asked Ginny, smiling at him.

All across London there was a hunt on for the two missing Luxbridge children. Posters were hung on every street corner, appealing for their safe return. Archibald and Mildred belonged to an upperclass family. They had gone missing from their home more than a week earlier. The police had questioned every thief and criminal in London in the hunt for them, to no avail. There was an offer of a reward for their safe return. Ginny could see that Theo was thinking about this as a smile crept across his lips.

"I want my sister," said the boy.

"She's safe, Archie."

"I've been trying to contact her with my mind, but there is no response, which means that Millie is either asleep or worst of all that she is dead!" Archie cried.

"You've been trying to contact her with your mind? What on earth does that mean?" Theo blurted out as Archie sobbed.

"Theo, please!" Ginny frowned, and two lines converged in the centre of her forehead.

"You heard him – he said he's been trying to contact

her with his mind. That means he has some sort of gift, like us."

How strange, thought Ginny.

"You don't think she's dead, do you?" Archie sat on the floor, small rivers of tears flowing from his eyes as he waited for Ginny's response. He could not imagine life without Millie. Although she was annoying as most sisters were, he loved her with all his heart and it was his job as her brother to take care of her.

Ginny felt sorry for Archie. She knew what it was like to feel alone, and hated to see him so sad. "Don't worry, Archie," she said. "Millie is quite safe. She's asleep in one of the cages outside. I saw her with my own two eyes. We need to get out of here and rescue her."

Archie stopped crying and looked at Ginny. He felt that he could trust her although he did not feel as certain about Theo.

"What about the old woman?" Theo asked.

"We'll have to wait for now. If we try to leave we won't get very far," Ginny said.

"But what about Millie?" Archie knew that the longer it took to reach his sister, the greater the danger she was in.

Theo sat back down on the rug and crossed his legs.

"We'll do it tonight, when the circus is over, and they're all in bed."

"What are you three whispering about?" the old woman snarled. She sprang up on the mattress, like a jack-in-the-box, and stuck her bony finger up her left nostril. A fly buzzed around her head.

"Nothing," said Ginny.

"Well, be warned – I have my eye on you three."

Chapter Four

The Great Circus Escape Plan

The circus slept and the magic that had captivated the audience only hours earlier had vanished beneath the stars like a dream. Theo had kept watch for hours, his eyes heavy with sleep. He stepped outside the tent and felt the misty rain on his skin. When the threat of danger did not seem apparent, he crept back inside the tent to wake Ginny and Archie.

Archie was sleeping with his head on Ginny's lap. She had fallen asleep propped up against the bookcase. Her long blonde hair fell in front of Archie's face like a curtain.

The old woman was snoring on the mattress. The dog was asleep at her feet.

Earlier in the night Theo had watched Badblood and Antonia go into a red tent across the field. The tent appeared to glow in the darkness as a candle flickered inside. He waited until the candle went out. Then he waited even longer. He waited until the lions had stopped roaring. He waited until the clowns had stopped laughing. And he waited until the moon was high in the sky.

Theo shook Ginny's shoulder. It took a moment for her to remember where she was. Then she looked at Archie, who was fast asleep. Even when he was sleeping he looked sad. His hand made the shape of a fist. One by one Ginny uncurled his fingers. Archie opened his eyes and jumped to his feet. Theo looked angry so Ginny put her finger to her lips to hush him. She knew Theo would leave the boy behind in a heartbeat if he caused them any trouble.

Theo walked out of the tent first. He looked right and left and, when he could see the coast was clear, he beckoned Ginny and Archie to follow him.

They ran across the field towards the cages and Ginny noticed the Siamese Twins walking towards them. There were two men with them, one at either side, linking their arms. They looked like sailors. They wore blue-and-white-striped T-shirts with white trousers. One of the men had a green scarf around his neck, and he was holding a bottle in his hand. Golden liquid sloshed around inside it.

Ginny pointed to them and Theo pulled her and Archie back behind a wooden storage crate. They waited in the shadows as the group approached. One of the women flicked open a fan and the other giggled. The sailor with the green scarf stooped to tie his shoelace. As he bent down, he looked straight into Ginny's eyes. He winked at her, stood up and walked away.

"Do you think he'll say anything?" Archie asked. His face was white with fear.

"We don't have time to find out. Come on." Theo led them to Millie's cage.

Ginny was happy to discover that the Elephant Man had gone.

Millie was standing up, her arms sticking out between the bars. Archie ran to his sister and took hold of her hands.

"We've come to rescue you, Millie – don't worry!"

Millie started to cry.

"*Shh!* Stop snivelling or they'll hear you," Theo hissed.

Millie fell silent as he opened the lock with the point of Badblood's knife. Then Ginny helped Millie down.

Together they made their way along a muddy part of the field and climbed over a fence into another field. It was filled with black-and-white cows, chewing on tufts of grass. They ran through the field until they came to a disused railway track.

Theo looked around.

"I think we should follow this track – it should lead us into the city."

I'm hungry, Archie, Millie, said to her brother in her mind.

Archie nodded at her, to let her know he understood.

Theo noticed that they were communicating. "Have you two always been able to thought-read?" he asked.

"Yes, we were born with it," said Millie. "We are able to speak to each other with our thoughts. At first people believed that it was because we were twins that we were so close. But as we got older our parents realised that we could talk to each other without even being in the same room."

Archie took his sister by the hand. "It used to work very well if we were playing hide and seek with our cousin George. Millie would run and hide in the maze and I could tell her when George was close to finding her so she could find another hiding place!"

Suddenly Millie began to feel quite weak.

"Is there any food?" she enquired. Her stomach was grumbling as she had not eaten in such a long time.

"We didn't have time to take any food," said Ginny. "But as soon as we reach the city we'll get something."

Millie nodded at her. She didn't know if she could make it as far as the city without something to eat.

Theo began to get frustrated with the Luxbridge twins. They were slowing him down. He knew that if they didn't hurry Badblood would find them, so he walked on ahead.

The railway track seemed to go on forever. Ginny

watched a mouse scuttling alongside the track, in the tall yellow grass. The wind whistled and blew through the branches of the trees. Two blackbirds with yellow eyes screeched at each other from the branches. They looked like old men, their feathers wrapped around their plump bodies like overcoats.

"My foot hurts," Millie said.

"Do you ever stop?" said Theo.

"Theo, if you want to get your hands on that reward, we'll have to take care of them," Ginny said, shaking her head. Although the money meant nothing to her, she feared that Theo would do anything to get his hands on it.

Theo smiled at Ginny and patted Archie on the head.

They walked on and on. Gradually the sky turned from black to blue as the rising sun illuminated it.

"Theo, look!" Ginny cried.

Further along the train track was an abandoned railway carriage. It was painted in red and green. The words 'Witcherly Sisters' were painted on the side in gold letters. There were six heart-shaped windows on either side of the carriage and the door also was heart-shaped. Each of the windows was covered in red-velvet curtains which had been pulled across, so the children couldn't see inside. The largest apple tree the children had ever seen grew out of the centre of the carriage. It burst through the roof like a giant. Ripe red apples, hanging from silver branches, shone in the sunlight. The sweet smell of the apples was intoxicating. There was a beehive on the roof of the carriage and Millie watched as the bees, drunk with honey, flew back and forth from the daffodils that lined the railway track. It looked so enticing.

"Perhaps we can rest in there for a while," Millie said, with her fingers crossed behind her back.

"All right then, but just for a while," Theo said. He was feeling hungry too and he could almost taste the juicy ripe apples – and a break was exactly what he needed, as he hadn't slept all night.

Archie and Millie disappeared through the heart-shaped door.

Ginny placed a hand on Theo's arm and looked into his eyes.

"Thank you, Theo."

"What for?"

"For taking care of me and Blue."

Theo smiled at Ginny. She was like a sister to him and he would always take care of her.

The wind had pulled some of the ripe apples from the branches, and they carpeted the field around the carriage. Small birds had pecked holes in them, and a worm wriggled out from underneath an apple core. The body of a dead sparrow lay beside it, its tiny legs pointed to the sky. Its wings were open wide, as though it were flying. Ginny looked away, glad that Blue hadn't seen the tiny dead bird.

She picked up two red apples. She handed one to Theo and bit into the other. The juice oozed from her mouth and ran down her chin.

Suddenly the sky grew dark and black clouds covered the sun. Ginny began to feel cold as the first raindrops fell.

She shouted Archie and Millie's names but they did not respond.

"Archie and Millie, come out here!" she shouted again, louder this time.

But there was still no response. As Ginny touched the door handle of the carriage, she had a bad feeling. The sky cracked open like an egg, and thunder shook the ground beneath their feet. Theo considered leaving the Luxbridge twins where they were – they were holding them back. Then he thought of the reward money and knew he would have to keep them close. He moved towards the door of the railway carriage.

Ginny pulled the door open and stepped into the carriage. It was dark inside. She saw something move in the shadows and tried to scream, but a gloved hand covered her mouth. She kicked her legs and thumped her fists but there was nothing she could do to warn Theo as he followed her into the dark carriage and straight into Badblood's fist.

Chapter Five

Cottonopolis

The circus travelled from town to town. The children were tired and hungry. They thought about trying to escape again in the middle of the night. But they decided that it would be pointless. Archie felt as though the moon was conspiring with Badblood as it winked down at the murky brown landscape.

Ginny was struck by how similar each town looked. Chocolate-coloured lanes that led to dull, box-shaped houses. The people were the same too. Wherever they went, they saw sunken grey faces with black slits of eyes. Poverty gripped the land like a fever. Even the trees and foliage appeared to be shrouded in a grey veil. Branches of trees hung like lifeless limbs from weather-beaten tree trunks. Thistles lined the murky undergrowth – cockroaches climbed their prickly leaves and danced on blades of yellow grass.

Then the circus arrived in Cottonopolis, as Manchester was often called. A grey sky loomed over the heads of the factory workers. They scurried like ants out of the warehouses and factories that lined the Bridgewater Canal. The clanging machines in the cotton mills conversed with the steam engines as they pulled into Liverpool Road Railway Station.

Millie stifled a cough with the back of her hand. The smog tickled her throat and the smell of smoke clung to her clothes. Amber sparks rose from the hot chimneystacks and set the grey sky on fire.

Millie watched the workers – men, women and children, their clothes covered in soot and dust. Their bloodshot eyes provided the only hint of colour in their grey faces.

A blind boy felt his way along the overcrowded street. His left arm was missing from the elbow down. Millie had heard that children were often injured when operating the spinning machines in the cotton mills. She stepped to one side to make way for him.

A crowd of Irish immigrants spilled off the steam train from Liverpool, their melodic voices filling the air. They spoke in a language she didn't understand. Millie had never seen people look so close to death before.

A woman cradled a baby in her arms. Her ribs were visible beneath her cotton dress. Her bare feet were dirty. Beside her were two more children, a girl with black hair like Millie's and a boy a year or two older with large blue eyes. He wore a flat cap and stared at the ground. His face was covered in fluid-filled blisters and he clung to his mother's skirt. Millie knew he had smallpox and she covered her face with her hand. The woman's husband was nowhere to be seen. Millie watched the family make their way towards a boarding house at the end of the dock. The boy tried to hide his face by pulling his cap down over his eyes.

A woman stood in the doorway of the boarding house, smoking a pipe. She had a large chest and a dimple in the centre of her chin. The smell of onions and bacon followed her out onto the docks.

"We need a room," the mother said with desperation in her voice. The baby began to cry, a painful cry.

Millie wondered if the baby was sick too.

"We don't serve your kind in here."

The woman pointed to a sign pinned to the door of the boarding house that read:

NO DOGS AND NO IRISH

The woman fell to her knees and the boy knelt down beside her, while the girl with the black hair stared at Millie.

Millie started to feel sick herself. She began to shiver and her throat was sore.

The sound of horse hoofs rang out on the cobbles, and Millie watched a hearse go by with a coffin inside. The horse was black apart from a white patch on its nose, and it had four big feathers secured to its head with a band. The crowd parted to make way for the funeral. The Irishmen stopped and waited for it to pass, while the women ran their fingers along wooden beads.

Millie felt a hand on her shoulder and it startled her.

"Millie, we've been looking for you," said Ginny. "The show is about to start."

Ginny's face looked flushed. "Come on!" She grabbed Millie by the hand and dragged her away.

They passed a pigsty that smelt like an overflowing privy and it made Millie want to vomit.

A respectable-looking man stood behind a wooden cart, selling potions. He wore a tall hat on his head. Millie considered asking him if he had a remedy to cure the boy with smallpox, but Ginny refused to stop.

Inside the backstage part of the tent, Theo was pacing up and down.

"I'm glad you decided to join us, Millie."

His sarcasm was apparent to Millie, who ran to Archie's side. She felt sick and her head ached. The children were to perform for the first time that night.

They stood behind the red-velvet curtain, which was drawn to the side. From there they had a view of the ring.

Antonia was strolling around there, with a black cane in her hand and a pink flower in her hair, when four extraordinarily muscular strongmen entered the tent. They pushed a long and incredibly tall cage into the centre of the ring. It was on four wheels and curtained with red-velvet cloth. The sound of a roar came from inside the cage and the audience gasped. The strongmen ran from the tent and Antonia walked over to the cage. Then she pulled a golden cord and the red-velvet cloth swished back on each side of the cage. Inside was the largest creature that Millie had ever seen. It had the head of a lion and the body of a tiger. It was a liger. Golden fur mottled with grey-and-black stripes covered its body. Millie's father had told her that a liger had been exhibited at the court of King William IV and of Queen Victoria, but she had never seen one before. It roared for the second time and revealed two large sharp teeth. As it reared up on its hind legs, the audience cowered in fright.

Elsewhere in the ring, a circus bear had a large metal chain around its neck. One of the circus clowns held onto the chain as the bear balanced a red ball on the tip of its nose. Clumps of its fur were missing and it looked inadequate next to the liger.

"Ready, children?"

Badblood had appeared at their side.

The sound of the crowd was deafening, and Millie shook with fright.

"It's all right, Millie." Archie held his sister's hand tight. He tried to act as though he wasn't scared, although he was petrified.

They all were, even Theo.

Badblood had warned them that they would be thrown into the Bridgewater Canal if they didn't perform well. They all knew that Badblood meant what he said. One of the clowns, a red-haired man called Rusty, had failed to make the crowd laugh one night and he was never seen again. Rumour had it that he was fed to the lions, and any bones that remained were crushed up and used for animal feed.

Antonia had disappeared and the liger and bear were taken inside.

The sound of the drumroll could be heard: *rat-a-tat-tat*, *rat-a-tat-tat!* Then silence. You could hear a pin drop as Badblood entered the ring.

He held a whip in his right hand and a gold pocket watch in his left. His red face looked shiny under the light. He introduced Antonia who entered the ring on the back of an elephant. The pearls on her bodice sparkled as she waved to the crowds. People gasped in astonishment as she stood on the elephant's back. Millie could see scars on the elephant's wrinkled skin from where it had been struck with Badblood's whip.

The elephant sucked up water from a tub with its trunk and then lifted the trunk high in the air and squirted water into the audience. Laughter erupted, then the elephant swished its tail and walked out of the ring. When the laughter subsided, Badblood spoke.

"Ladies and gentlemen, welcome to the Greatest Show on Earth! You are about to witness death-defying stunts, a Bearded Lady, an Elephant Man, the Two-Headed Lady from Siam. As well as Tom Thumb and Thumbelina, the smallest man and woman in the history of the world! But first, allow me to introduce to you to the Most Magnificent Children on Earth. *Drumroll, please!*"

"Archie, I can't do it," Millie cried. A pain shot through her stomach.

A black hair was stuck to her lip. Archie picked it off.

"Just do what we rehearsed," he said.

Two clowns with painted faces and large trousers opened the red-velvet curtains. Theo was scared that Millie would spoil things, so he stepped into the ring first.

He had never revealed his gift to people before and, if he had the choice, he would not have done it now. However, he knew there was no other way. His heart thumped in his chest as he looked around the ring at the sea of faces that stared back at him. He felt faint.

"What's so magnificent about him?"

"Yeah, he's just a lad."

The crowd heckled. They hissed, booed and spat at him.

Theo closed his eyes tight and concentrated as hard as he could. He knew that it was now or never.

Moments later a woman in the back row screamed. Theo looked down and realised that his feet had risen eight inches off the ground. He smiled with delight, then he folded his arms across his chest and floated across the ring.

"*He's tied up with rope!*" someone cried.

"*Yeah, it's a trick!*"

"*I want my money back!*"

Theo began to wobble and, for a moment, he thought he would fall to the ground. But then Ginny appeared. The audience was captivated by her beauty. The crown of green silk flowers on her head made her appear like royalty.

In her hand was a wooden hoop, decorated with purple and pink ribbons. Ginny placed the hoop over Theo's head and ran it along his body and under his feet. The crowd clapped and cheered and Ginny felt relieved.

Theo carefully lowered himself to the ground and revealed his second gift. He knew he was taking a risk, and that he might frighten people as he had in the past. He walked over to the audience and picked a woman from the front row. A yellow bonnet was balanced precariously on her head. The woman was delighted. She fluttered her butterfly-shaped eyelashes at Theo and blushed. The skin on her neck matched the colour of the ribbon. She wore an emerald ring on each finger. The green stones sparkled under the light. Theo considered stealing the rings from her. However, her fingers were shaped like sausages and he knew that getting the rings off would be a struggle.

Theo led the woman to the centre of the ring, pointed to a three-legged stool and instructed the woman to sit on it. The crowd laughed as the stool disappeared from view beneath her dress.

"What's he doing?"

"Do you think he'll make her fly?"

Theo looked into the woman's blue eyes. He held up his left hand to silence the audience. Not a sound could be heard apart from the occasional cough or nervous giggle.

Theo knew that for his gift to work he would have to concentrate hard and block out all the sounds around him. After a few minutes he opened his mouth and it looked as though he was about to sing. But an extraordinary thing happened, and the crowd were amazed.

A woman's voice came out of Theo's mouth. It was quiet at first, so quiet that you would have to strain to hear it. But then the voice grew louder and louder, so loud in fact that the people in the front row had to cover their ears with their hands. The woman's words flew out of Theo's mouth like a swarm of bees.

"I am scared of birds. I always think that they're going to peck my one good eye out!"

The crowd began to laugh.

"My worst fear is that my husband will find out about my glass eye!"

The woman's voice got louder and Theo's mouth opened wide. So wide in fact that people could see his tonsils swaying back and forth like the pendulum in a grandfather clock.

When the woman's voice stopped, a gust of wind blew out of Theo's mouth and made his lips quiver. The woman's bonnet blew off her head and landed on the head of a young boy with freckles in the second row.

The woman thought things couldn't possibly get any worse but then Theo's eyelids flickered and he looked as though he were having a bad dream. Beads of perspiration lined his forehead. The audience became uneasy when he fell to his knees and then stretched out and wriggled like a snake on the floor.

"He doesn't look well."

"Someone call a doctor!"

But then a drumbeat sounded somewhere off stage: *rat-a-tat-tat, rat-a-tat-tat!* The crowd were silent again and Theo stopped wriggling. He stood up in front of the woman and pulled her to her feet. His eyes were shut as he took her hands and leant in close. So close that she could feel his breath on her cheek – and then their foreheads were touching.

Theo's eyelids sprang open like trapdoors and his eyeballs began to grow in size until his eyes were the size of large dinner plates.

The spectators looked on as a horrifying image was projected up into the air. The image came from Theo's eyes and it hung above their heads like a dark cloud on a summer's day.

The image was of the woman: she was sitting in a rocking chair in front of a fire, knitting a scarf and whistling a tune. On her hands she wore black fingerless mittens, and a brown shawl covered her shoulders. Without any warning she dropped her knitting onto the floor, slumped over the edge of her rocking chair and died.

The crowd began to shout and scream when they realised that Theo had the ability to see how people would die.

The woman placed her sausage-shaped fingers in her ears, screamed at the top of her lungs and ran out of the tent.

Using his gift in this way left Theo feeling exhausted and he stumbled out of the ring.

Ginny looked at Millie who had started to cough loudly. Ginny realised that she would have to perform next although she suddenly felt unwell. She was aware that she would have to do her best as her own life, and the lives of her friends, depended on it.

Chapter six

Liverpool
The Floating Circus

The ship arrived at the dock in Liverpool as the orange sun began to sink in the sky. Seagulls squawked overhead, then swooped down to scavenge for any scraps of food that they could find.

The smell of fish rose from a fishing trawler that had just docked. Four men in brown overcoats and flat caps lowered cargo onto a barge. Then the thick knotted rope that they were holding gave way and the cargo landed in the water with a splash.

A row of black and brown suitcases containing the circus performers' costumes lined the docks. Badblood had insisted that they move from Manchester three days earlier to catch the ship to Ireland. The Siamese Twins were arguing with a man who refused to carry their luggage on board. Antonia sat on top of a black suitcase with a red-and-white scarf tied around it. Her legs dangled over the edge of the dock. Her cheeks were covered in white powder and her eyes sparkled like bubbles in a glass of champagne. She was talking to a sailor with a large forehead and a black beard. She threw her head back and laughed as he whispered into her ear.

Millie stood on the dock and shivered. She coughed into a small white handkerchief that Ginny had given her. Antonia's name was embroidered in the corner in gold thread. Droplets of blood appeared on the handkerchief like red ink. When Millie noticed the blood, she discreetly folded the handkerchief and placed it into the pocket of her dress. Archie noticed that his sister's condition was deteriorating and he was worried that Millie would not survive the treacherous journey across the Irish Sea. He knew better than to tell anyone about Millie's sickness or she would end up in the Cholera Pit. So many people were dying from the cholera epidemic that they had created mass graves known as pits. Archie was determined that Millie was not going to end up in the pit. He shuddered at the thought of losing his twin sister. He knew that Millie was able to read his mind and he didn't want her to detect his sadness, so he tried to think of something else instead. He sat Millie down on a crate to rest, then sat beside her and put his arm protectively around her.

The animals boarded the ship first. They went on the lower deck. They were kept inside their cages at all times for the safety of other passengers. The animals had kept the children awake the night before. It was as though they had sensed that they were going on a journey.

The liger paced up and down in his cage. He nudged the bars with his head to try and break free.

Then the old elephant with the sad black eyes managed to escape. One of the clowns hadn't locked its cage properly. The animal went wild. He raised his trunk in the air and ran up onto the deck of the ship. Despite the best efforts of the deckhands to try and restrain him, within seconds he thundered off the boat and headed down the overcrowded dock. It was busier than usual. People were buying ferry tickets and men were queuing up in a desperate attempt to secure a job on board the boat.

Men, women and children ran away in fear. They screamed and shouted as the elephant hurtled towards them. Badblood and one of the circus hands tried to drive him back. They struck him with steel bars and the elephant hook which dug into his flesh, but he was much too strong and pushed them away.

He almost trampled on a poor boy called Charlie Climber, a ten-year-old chimney sweep, but a man selling newspapers dragged the boy away just in time. Charlie was sleeping outside a grocery store, on top of a bag of soot that he had collected earlier in the day. He was a friendly boy, always smiling. He explained to Archie and Millie one day how he climbed up inside the hot sooty chimneys and cleaned the inside of the flues with a wire brush. His job was hazardous and he had a twisted spine and his eyes were always red.

Badblood and the circus hand, eventually, managed to restrain the elephant.

The crowd of people that gathered on the dock were outraged over what had nearly happened to Charlie. Millie thought that if they had cared enough about Charlie, he would not have been sweeping chimneys and lying out on the street in the first place.

Archie and Millie had witnessed the whole thing as they had lingered on the dock after the others had boarded. They were horrified but relieved that Charlie had survived. They ran as quickly as they could to tell the others what had happened. But Millie was overcome with dizziness halfway up the gangway. She staggered and all but fell into the water but Archie grabbed her around the waist in time. He helped her on board. Millie could still hear the sound of the elephant's roar ringing out in the night's sky as the hook dug into its hide.

Below decks there was barely room to move. There were only a small number of wooden benches so people huddled together on flea-ridden blankets on the floor. Archie and Millie found Theo and Ginny lying on some filthy blankets with the old woman with the bulging eyes and the Siamese Twins. The old woman said that it was a sign. She said that the elephant had sensed trouble and that they would all die in the Irish Sea.

Archie made sure that Millie lay down on the blanket farthest from the old woman. He lay down beside her and shielded her from view.

Conditions were far worse than anyone had expected. The smell was foul. Archie knew it was because the animals were kept with the people. The stench of horse dung and vomit filled the air.

Ginny noticed Antonia sitting on a bench talking to Badblood. She felt anger turn like a screw in her heart as she stood up and glared at them.

"Where are you going, Ginny? Sit down," Theo warned.

But Ginny ignored him and walked defiantly over to where Badblood and Antonia were sitting.

"We are too cramped – there is not enough room for us down here," Ginny complained.

"Well, I can soon fix that problem." Badblood laughed a deep, guttural laugh that came from the pit of his stomach.

Then he gestured to two of the clowns, a double act called Mr Feather Brain and Silly Sam, who were trying to settle the animals.

"Come here, boys – this young lady says that there isn't enough room for her on board. Perhaps she would prefer to be in the vast expanse of the sea? Could you take her to walk the plank, please?"

"We don't have a plank!" one of the clowns replied, while the other one hit him on the back of the head.

In any other circumstance their double act would have caused Ginny to laugh but she suddenly realised that she was in great danger.

"Wait, there is no need to overreact, my dearest." Antonia placed her hand on Badblood's arm as she spoke. "Ginny was only joking – isn't that right, Ginny?"

Ginny nodded. She was grateful to Antonia for intervening and wished that she had not approached Badblood.

"The Siamese Twins don't take up too much room, do they, cherub?" said Antonia. "Why, they have only one body between them. Now go and sit down, there's a good girl."

Then she placed her arms around Badblood's neck and winked at Ginny.

Ginny went and sat down beside Theo who elbowed her in the ribs.

"What are you playing at? You nearly got yourself killed and us along with you!"

The waves were choppy and the ship rocked back and forth. The children started to itch – it seemed that the lice were hungry. They could be seen hopping from one person to the next.

There was a narrow gangway down the centre of

the ship; it was always wet as urine sloshed along it. The buckets that they used as toilets overflowed. The girls had to hold up their dresses to prevent them from getting wet. It was so dark below deck that the children could not tell whether it was night or day.

They were given water biscuits to eat. They were as hard as rocks and as dry as sand. Theo broke his front tooth trying to chew on one. The biscuits were infested with maggots. Weevils, small white insects, wriggled their soft cream bodies and looked as though they were dancing inside the food. The children refused to touch them at first but, as sharp pains darted across their stomachs, they realised that they had no choice but to try and force the maggot-infested food down as there was nothing else to eat.

Archie held Millie close, but she was getting weaker. Puss-filled welts appeared on her legs and Archie feared that she had somehow contracted smallpox. Then halfway across the Irish Sea she broke out in a fever. Large droplets of sweat gathered on her forehead and ran down her skin, which was cold to the touch and covered in goose bumps. Ginny saw the petrified look on Archie's face and the dark shadows that had formed beneath his eyes.

Archie looked over at the old woman – she had pulled her black shawl over her face and she was snoring. He showed Ginny the bloodstained handkerchief.

Ginny then realised how sick Millie had become. She knew that it would only be a matter of time before Badblood noticed and Millie would be flung overboard like a dead fish just as he had wanted to do with her earlier.

"How long has she been like this, Archie?" Ginny whispered while placing her hand on Millie's brow.

"Since before we left Liverpool." Archie looked at Ginny in despair as Millie began to cough again. Her lips were dry and cracked.

"Does anyone else know that she is sick?"

"I don't think so."

"Good. We'll have to keep it that way."

The old woman turned over on the blanket and the children waited until they heard her snore again.

"I will have to go up on deck and try and get some water for Millie," Ginny whispered. "There isn't any left down here."

"But, Ginny, what if someone sees you?"

"We have no choice, Archie. Without water Millie will die."

Ginny knew that she was risking her life going onto the upper deck – she had already upset Badblood once that day – but in the absence of any medicine she knew that Millie needed something to drink and fast.

When she was certain that everyone was asleep, she walked softly along the gangway.

She stopped at the first cage she passed and looked

in through the bars at the brown bear. A fly buzzed around its head. She put her hand through the bars and stroked the animal. It moved its head towards her and poked a small pink tongue out of its mouth. Ginny could see that the bear was thirsty too. Its fur felt so soft between her fingertips. Ginny realised that in many ways she was no different from the brown bear. She too had been captured by the circus and made to perform. She had no more control over her future than the sad-looking bear.

She heard the sound of footsteps in the darkness and thought that she was being followed. She hid behind the cage until a man in a purple coat and striped trousers went past. Ginny recognised him as one of the clowns. When the coast was clear, she ran over to the wooden ladders and climbed onto the deck.

The upper deck was crowded with people too. Ginny saw bodies lying everywhere in the moonlight. She stepped over the arms and legs of men, women and children. She took a deep breath and filled her lungs with fresh air. Blue flew around inside her. The stench on the lower deck had been unbearable.

Ginny gripped the side of the ship and stared at the black waves as they licked at the boat. She imagined brightly coloured fish swimming beneath the sea. Yellow starfish and green seahorses. She saw a shape in the distance. She envisaged a whale or perhaps a beautiful mermaid perched on a rock, with a green scaled tail attached to a milky-white body. Ginny imagined the mermaid combing her golden hair as it tumbled over her freckled shoulders. She thought of her singing a magical song that would lure unsuspecting sailors to their deaths.

Steam from the engine cast a fog into the night sky. Ginny looked up at the stars; she had never seen so many stars before. The full moon beamed down – it looked as though it was following them across the sea.

The sound of music came from the far end of the ship. Ginny walked towards it. She stood beside a wooden barrel containing rope. Her feet ached with tiredness, so she leant against the barrel and placed her hand beneath her chin.

There were three musicians.

One was an old Jewish man wearing a skullcap, with a long black beard. Curls framed his square jaw. He wore a white shirt and his sleeves were rolled up. On the bridge of his nose sat a pair of spectacles. He played the accordion and smiled at Ginny.

A girl with black cropped hair played the tin whistle. She had large bushy eyebrows that met in the centre of her forehead. She wore a long straight red dress with puffed sleeves.

The final musician played the violin. She recognised him from the party at Antonia's house. His face was shaped like the moon. It was Mr Moonshine. He winked at her and she blushed.

The music was like nothing else she had ever heard before. People were dancing hornpipes and jigs.

Two young women hitched their skirts up above their knees so that you could see their drawers. The first woman was wearing a dirty green dress; the hem was torn and her feet were bare, her ankles brown. The second woman had a head of blonde curls and bright red cheeks – she had a black mole on her neck and her shabby brown dress looked out of place on her. Ginny thought that the women looked very beautiful and that they would be better suited to a dancehall in Paris or London. They linked arms and danced in circles. They were spinning around so fast Ginny could not understand how they didn't fall over.

Then one of the women spied Ginny out of the corner of her eye and they danced towards her. The blonde woman, who had emerald-green eyes, the colour of the flowers on Ginny's crown, grabbed her by the waist, took hold of her right arm and waltzed with her across the deck. Ginny laughed as the crowd around them clapped their hands and stomped their feet in time to the music. For a moment Ginny forgot where she was, and began to enjoy herself. Then the ship went over a huge wave and Ginny fell to the ground. Her dancing partner fell on top of her. Ginny had never laughed so much. The music continued to play and a man with a large nose handed her a bottle with golden liquid inside. Ginny put the bottle to her lips and drank, then she spluttered and coughed as she realised that the bottle contained whisky. The people around her howled with laughter.

Ginny lay back and looked up at the stars as her head spun. Then she remembered Millie lying sick below deck and jumped to her feet.

"Going so soon, are we?"

Mr Moonshine was standing in front of her, his violin in his left hand.

"I have to get back to my friend."

"Ah, the sick girl."

"How did you know?"

"I spotted her brother helping her onto the ship."

"Please don't tell anyone."

"She has the look of death on her, that one."

"If you tell she will be thrown overboard."

"She's putting all our lives in danger. She might infect us all."

Ginny noticed a large water barrel with a ladle on top of it. She moved towards it and Mr Moonshine grabbed her wrist.

"Please just give me until tomorrow night," Ginny pleaded. "She'll be better by then, I promise."

The man looked into Ginny's eyes. She was a beautiful girl and he hated to see her so sad.

"I have an idea," he said. "Bring the girl to me right away. I think I might be able to cure her."

"But how?"

"Don't ask questions, girl, just do as I say. You'll find me at the far end of the ship. What are you waiting for?"

Mr Moonshine loosened his grip on Ginny's wrist.

She hoped that it wasn't a trick. What if he was leading them to Badblood? And yet she knew that they had to trust him – what choice did they have? This could be Millie's last chance.

Ginny climbed back down the ladders. It took a moment for her eyes to adjust to the darkness and she had to fight the urge to vomit as the smell of urine filled her nostrils.

As she approached the others, she saw that the old woman with the bulging eyes was gone. The Siamese Twins lay sleeping beside Theo, who had his arms folded across his chest. A line of dribble had escaped from the corner of his mouth and dripped onto his chin.

But Archie was awake, waiting for her.

"Where has the old witch gone?" Ginny whispered.

"I don't know – she left shortly after you."

"We have to get Millie up onto the deck, Archie. She'll die here."

"What if someone sees us?"

"It's her only hope, Archie. I met someone who said he can help her."

"Who?"

"Mr Moonshine."

"Badblood's musician? No, Ginny! It's a trap."

"We have no choice, Archie, and little time to lose."

"I don't know."

"Trust me, Archie."

Archie moved over towards Millie, who was fast asleep. Her face was dripping with sweat and her hair was wet.

Archie knew that Ginny was right. He didn't think that Millie would survive the night.

Although Millie was as light as a feather and her narrow bones protruded through her dress, Archie wasn't strong enough to carry her, so Ginny lifted Millie in her arms and carried her with great difficulty up the ladders and onto the deck while Archie followed close behind.

The music had ceased now and the ship was in darkness. Ginny retraced her footsteps. Her heart was thumping in her chest and she hoped that she was making the right decision. She was glad that Theo hadn't woken as he didn't care about the twins and she was afraid that he would try to persuade her not to help Millie. Ginny also realised that their chances of getting a reward for the safe return of the Luxbridge children were slim now that they had left England and it would be much more difficult to persuade Theo to care for them now.

Ginny carried Millie along the deck. It was much harder for her to keep her balance when she was holding the girl in her arms.

Ginny saw that a small red tent had been erected at

the end of the ship and Mr Moonshine was standing in the entrance. He bent his middle finger and beckoned the children towards him.

"This way, hurry."

He took Millie from Ginny's arms and carried her inside.

Inside, the tent was illuminated with candles.

The man who had played the accordion earlier was sitting cross-legged on a patterned rug with a glass jar in his hand. It contained strange black objects. Ginny thought back to the jars that she had seen in Antonia's room: one had contained a brain and the others deformed animals.

Then she saw the old woman with the bulging eyes also sitting there with her legs crossed, smoking a clay pipe.

Archie panicked when he saw the old woman.

"It's a trick! Quick, Ginny, help me!"

He grabbed Millie's lifeless arm and tried to pull her away from Mr Moonshine. The girl gave a small whimper.

The old woman's eyes bulged farther and farther from their sockets until they fell out and rolled across the rug. They stopped at Archie's feet.

Archie was unable to move. He stood still as a statue and did not say another word.

"We won't hurt any of you," the man with the glass jar in his hand said.

"This is Mr Leech," Mr Moonshine said to Ginny.

The old woman got up, picked her eyeballs up off the floor and popped them back into their sockets. Then she scattered some cushions on the rug and Mr Moonshine gently lay Millie down on them.

As if by magic, Archie was able to move again, but he knew better than to say anything this time. He moved over towards Ginny and they both sat down on the rug beside Millie.

Mr Leech placed his hand into the jar and Ginny watched in amazement as hundreds of shiny leeches the colour of treacle climbed onto it.

He pulled his hand out of the jar. Then he walked over to Millie, who was fast asleep on the cushions. He lifted her dress up to her knees. Ginny gasped as she saw the inflamed blisters on Millie's legs. Archie wiped a tear from his eye with the back of his wrist. Mr Leech knelt down and one by one he pulled the leeches off his hand and placed them on Millie's legs. The leeches began to suck the blood from Millie's skin.

"Stop, you're hurting her!" Archie pleaded.

"It's all right, Archie – we can trust them. They're helping Millie," Ginny soothed him. Then she reached over and held his hand.

He looked at her, his eyes wide in disbelief. "How can you say that, Ginny? The leeches are sucking her blood!"

When Mr Leech had placed the last of the black leeches on Millie's legs, he turned to Archie.

"You should listen to your friend, boy. These leeches are the only thing that can cure your sister now. But we will have to wait until morning to see if they take the infection away."

Archie rubbed Millie's forehead. The sweat was trickling down her neck.

"Archie, we have to go below deck now," said Ginny. "If Badblood discovers that we're here he will have us all killed."

"We can't leave Millie here – she might wake up," he said.

"She won't wake tonight," Mr Leech said. "Her fever is too high. I will keep watch tonight, boy."

As Mr Moonshine began to play a melancholy tune on his violin, Archie pointed to the old woman. "What about her? She'll tell Badblood." A streak of dirt had formed on his cheek but the gold buttons on his red coat shone in the candlelight.

"Don't worry about me, boy," said the old woman. "I'm just a foolish old woman with eyes that see only what they want to see."

"Come on, Archie, we have to go." Ginny stood up and took hold of Archie's hand. "Thank you," she said to Mr Leech who thought that Ginny was the most beautiful girl he had ever seen.

"You are welcome, girl. Here, take this." He handed

Ginny a black rose. The petals had wilted.

Ginny wondered where he had got a black rose from as she smiled at him.

Archie and Ginny stepped out of the tent and onto the deck. The waves were choppy and now and then a rogue wave stretched its white foamy fingers onto the ship. They stepped over the tangled bodies of men, women and children who clung to each other for warmth.

They saw a man being flung overboard. He must have died during the voyage.

They scurried along the deck and then climbed down the ladders and hurried along the narrow gangway.

They quietly lay back down on the blankets. The Siamese Twins were sleeping with their knees pulled up to their chest. Theo was still asleep, a trail of dribble still falling from his chin.

"Look, Ginny," Archie whispered.

Ginny's eyes took a moment to adjust to the darkness, but when they did she could not believe what she was seeing. The old woman with the bulging eyes was lying there fast asleep.

"How did she do that, Archie?"

"I don't know. There's no way that she could have got back down here before us."

Ginny's eyes were drooping with tiredness, and the motion of the waves rocked her to sleep. She dreamt of Mr Moonshine playing his violin. Millie was dressed as a ballerina and Mr Leech twirled her around and around. Millie looked so happy and somehow Ginny knew that the little girl was going to survive.

Chapter seven

Dublin
Billy Beak and the Wicked Children

A hint of magic clung to the stars that sparkled like diamonds in the sky. Men with monocles and top-hats accompanied ladies with lace gloves and parasols to their seats. The smell of boot polish and cigar smoke moved through the air.

A new department store called Brown Thomas had opened that day on Grafton Street, and the Dublin aristocrats were keen to display their sense of style at the circus. Each of the ladies wore a gorgeous bonnet on her head, some decorated with ribbons and bows and others with flowers – yellow roses and pink peonies. They held their heads high and looked around the tent enviously, hoping that they were the best dressed.

One woman wore a green silk dress, with long sleeves

– it was buttoned down the front and there was a large green bow around her waist. She wore green lace fingerless gloves. Another wore a white fox-fur stole around her neck, and long earrings shaped like daggers. But the most spectacularly dressed was a lady who wore a hat made out of purple and blue peacock feathers. Around her neck swung a pendant shaped like a heart.

Alongside the elite of the city sat every thief and pickpocket in Dublin. They worked in gangs and strategically placed themselves in the audience. They too could not wait for the circus to commence so that they could steal from the wealthy.

Even Badblood and Antonia were happy. They danced around in the Hall of Mirrors while they waited for the circus to commence. The Hall of Mirrors was a magical mirrored tent where a thin person would appear fat, a fat person would appear thin, a short person skinny and tall and a tall person dumpy and short. They had great fun looking at their distorted reflections.

When Badblood and Antonia at last emerged, Mr Moonshine began to play his violin, which indicated to the other performers that the circus was about to commence. He winked at Ginny as he had done on the ship.

A tightrope had been hung across the Big Top and Balancing Betty was walking across it in silver shoes with the greatest of ease. Millie covered her eyes as the rope was thin as a hair. Then the other performers entered and paraded around the ring. There were fire-eaters and sword-swallowers, lion tamers and human cannonballs. The world's strongest man lifted Antonia with one hand.

The Siamese Twins were the last to enter the tent. They wore a wonderful scarlet kimono and they had someone with them, a new performer all set to make his debut performance that night.

His name was Billy Beak. He was a short man with the face of a duck. He was brought in to replace the Elephant Man who had disappeared when they left Manchester. Billy Beak had a yellow beak where his nose should have been, his face was covered in coarse white feathers, and he waddled when he walked. He also had a stumpy tail. Billy Beak wore a tuxedo and a dickie bow. A hole had been cut out of his trousers to accommodate his tail which wagged whenever he walked. Mr Beak had assured Mr Badblood that he was not new to circus life. On the contrary, he had been born in the circus, and had travelled all over the world – from Africa to Singapore. But he always preferred to work at home in Ireland. He had a Dublin accent and smoked a cigar. He performed magic tricks that made the children laugh. Blue had taken quite a shine to Billy Beak, and Ginny had a hard time convincing her little feathered friend to get back into the birdcage whenever Billy Beak was around.

Badblood allowed Billy Beak to open the show. A ripple of excitement went through the audience as the other performers withdrew from the tent and Billy Beak took centre stage. The crowd laughed at his jokes and he somersaulted out of the ring to a standing ovation.

The children were up next. Badblood decided that they should all perform together. Archie could not help but smile. He did not care what he had to do – he was just glad that Millie was still alive. Although she wasn't fully recovered, he was relieved that she was over the worst of it now.

Badblood stepped into the ring.

"Ladies and Gentlemen, allow me to introduce to you four of the most magical creatures you will ever encounter! They can enter your minds, read your thoughts and even see how and when you will die! What kind of creatures can do such things, I hear you cry! Allow me to introduce to you: *Badblood's Magnificent Children!*"

Archie, Ginny and Theo entered the ring.

Ginny coughed, opened her mouth wide and stuck out her tongue. Then Blue appeared and flew around the tent, much to the amazement of the crowd who clapped and cheered. Theo closed his eyes and concentrated as hard as he could until his feet began to lift from the ground. He continued to move up until he was about two feet in the air.

Archie spoke through his mind to Millie, who was waiting in a small tent at the back of the ring.

"They are ready for you now, Millie – don't be scared."

Millie sniffed the ground and followed her brother's scent to the main ring. Then she walked in and looked around.

"Look, Mammy, it's a fox!" cried a small boy in the third row.

Millie walked over to Archie's side, and Archie stroked her red fur until she began to relax. Then she walked around the ring. She enjoyed being a fox. She could slip into places unnoticed and do things that she could not do as a child. Of course she had to be careful – she nearly got shot by a farmer once and another time her leg had got stuck in a trap. Archie had rescued her on both occasions.

Millie ran towards Archie, who was kneeling down. He held his arms open and smiled at her. Then just as she reached him she turned from a fox into a little girl.

The crowd were outraged.

"What kind of magic is this?" the woman wearing the fox stole shouted from the back of the audience. She took the dead fox from her neck and shook it at Millie.

"These are wicked children!" another man roared.

The children felt scared. Theo lowered himself to the ground. They had never performed in front of such a hostile crowd before. Ginny ran over to Theo as his two feet landed on the ground.

"Use your other gift, Theo!"

"Are you crazy, Ginny? They will kill us."

"We have to do something."

Ginny looked over to the side of the ring. Badblood stood there with a face like thunder. The whip in his hand cracked through the air.

Theo walked through the audience and selected the woman with the hat made from peacock feathers. A row of orange curls dangled beneath her hat. Her eyes were outlined in black pencil and she looked like an Egyptian princess. Her bow-shaped lips were painted red, and she smelt of lavender. On her legs were red stockings and dainty black shoes sat on her plump feet. Her dress was gold and low-cut and the heart-shaped pendant glittered under the lights.

Theo picked her as she looked like a woman who craved attention, and thankfully he was right.

"Come with me, madam," he said as he led her through the angry mob and into the centre of the ring.

The woman felt special. She was delighted to have been chosen over all the other women there.

Badblood was no longer standing at the side of the ring. Theo looked around. To his horror he saw Badblood just inside one of the red-velvet curtains, holding Millie in his arms. He had a knife with an ivory handle pressed against her pale throat and Theo knew that if he did not impress the crowd, Millie would pay the price.

"You have beautiful eyes," he said to the woman, who fluttered her eyelids in response. "May I look into them?"

"Yes, you may," the woman said coyly, pouting her lips at Theo.

Theo shut his eyes and concentrated hard for a few moments. He tried to think of the woman, but all he could see in his mind was Ginny. He opened his eyes and looked straight at the woman. Theo expected to see the woman's death in her eyes and to hear her innermost fears come tumbling from her lips. But instead the most extraordinary thing happened.

Theo looked into the woman's eyes and they gradually became larger and larger until they became as large as dinner plates – just as his usually did. Then an image appeared in the woman's eyes and was projected mid-air onto a cloud that appeared from nowhere. The audience were astonished and so was Theo. The image in the centre of the cloud was of Ginny. Ginny on the day he had found her lying in the white snow in a pool of blood. Ginny when she introduced him to the little blue bird who lived inside her ribcage, and Ginny smiling as they counted the coins that they had begged on the streets of London. The perplexed audience looked on in amazement at the scenes that flashed in front of them.

The next image that Theo saw came from Ginny's future. There was an old rundown house in a forest with crooked trees, and two women with long black hair.

Ginny was standing at the ringside and could see the images of her life flashing in front of her, although she did not understand what was happening. She stepped into the ring so that she could get a closer look.

Then a mini-tornedo swirled out of the woman's mouth. It was so intense that her lips trembled and her teeth shook. Theo fell to the ground and covered his eyes with his hand as a cloud of dust formed and spun across the tent.

When the wind had died down words tumbled from the woman's red lips.

"Theo, help me!" It was Ginny's voice.

"Enough!" shouted Theo. Then he clapped his hands and large silver raindrops fell from the cloud and onto the heads of the audience. When he looked up the cloud had gone.

Theo was relieved: he did not want to see how Ginny was going to die.

The audience gasped in amazement as the woman ran back to her seat.

Badblood loosened his grip from around Millie's neck as Theo ran over to Ginny who was as white as a ghost.

"I don't understand what just happened!" Ginny cried. She was overcome with fear and anxiety.

"Pay no attention, Ginny – my mind was playing tricks on me. That isn't going to happen."

"But that house, the forest with the crooked trees and the two wicked women. Do they really exist, Theo?"

Ginny was pleading with Theo and asking him questions that he did not know the answers to. But he realised that he had to reassure her. She was still pale as a ghost, her blonde hair falling across her face and framing her beautiful features like golden curtains. The green flowers on her crown appeared to be wilting although Theo knew that this could not be possible as they were made from silk. Theo moved so close to her that he could feel her breath on his cheek. Then he caught her just in time as she trembled and fainted into his arms.

Chapter eight

Wexford, Ireland
The Vanishing Circus

When Ginny woke up, the circus had gone.

She looked around in disbelief. All that she could see were the green fields, a forest, and rolling hills that looked like sleeping giants. Four black-and-white cows chewed yellow tufts of grass. They raised their weary heads in Ginny's direction, nodded and looked away.

There were large holes in the grass where the tent pegs had been. Ginny placed her finger into one of the holes and clawed at the soil with her nails. A blackbird spotted a worm wriggling in the soil. It cut the worm in half with its sharp beak and flew back to its nest.

Ginny cried with delight as she realised that she was free at last. The lions and tigers, the fire-breathers, and the sword-swallowers had all gone. The candy-cane-coloured tent, the Siamese Twins with their pale faces and twinkling eyes, even Billy Beak – they had all disappeared like a bad dream.

Ginny ran over to where the children lay. They had fallen asleep around a campfire and still lay sleeping beneath three scratchy blankets.

"Wake up, Theo, wake up!"

"What is it?" Millie asked.

Archie looked at Ginny. He was still half asleep, and he rubbed his eyes with the back of his hand and yawned.

"What is all this commotion about? Let me sleep!" Theo muttered then rolled over onto his side.

"Theo, Badblood's circus has gone! We're free!"

"Is this your idea of a joke, Ginny? It's not funny."

Theo jumped to his feet. His shirt had ridden up at the back and Ginny noticed a small red scab where Badblood's knife had stabbed him. Then he picked up the small cloth bag which contained all of his worldly possessions and ran towards the forest in his bare feet.

Ginny and the twins ran after him.

Theo turned at the edge of the forest and waited for them.

"I don't believe it, Ginny! We're free at last."

Ginny had never seen Theo so excited before and she smiled with delight. Archie and Millie skipped around in circles.

"Let's get on the next boat back to England," said Theo.

Suddenly Millie screamed. It was a piercing scream – the kind you might reserve for seeing a monster in the dark. She had noticed the figure of a person walking between the trees. As fear took hold she ran over to Ginny and hid behind her back. Theo dropped the cloth bag that he was holding, and a photograph of Ginny slid out onto the ground.

A gloved hand waved at them from behind a tree and the children's hearts sank as Badblood appeared.

He tipped his hat to them. "You didn't think we'd left you all alone, did you? I sent the others on ahead. I wanted to stay and take care of you."

As he spoke he stepped close to Ginny and ran his fingers across her lips. They smelt of whisky and tobacco and Ginny pulled away.

"Answer me, girl." He wrapped a strand of Ginny's hair around his finger and yanked her head back. "Did you think we'd left you all alone?"

"No, we didn't, Mr Badblood!" Ginny cried.

"Good." He released the strand of hair. "Remember I'll always be there to take care of you." He pointed across the field to where a horse and cart was approaching, Antonia sitting in front. "Here she is!"

He walked off to meet the cart.

Hot angry tears were falling from Millie's eyes.

"You said we were free! It's all your fault!" She ran over to Ginny and punched her hard in the chest with her small fists. Then she kicked her in the shin.

"*Stop that, Millie!*" Theo grabbed Millie and threw her onto the grass.

Ginny was shocked and hurt by Theo's aggressive behaviour. She walked over and hugged Millie. The young girl felt so frail and delicate in her arms it was as though she were made of porcelain.

"*I don't believe you, Ginny! Why are you so good to her?*"

"If you think that things are hard for us, then imagine how hard it is for Archie and Millie. They are not used to living like this."

"*I don't want anything to do with you two, do you hear me?*" Theo shouted at Archie and Millie, who were now huddled together shaking. Then he stormed off into the forest.

Ginny followed him through the trees and placed her hand on his shoulder. He pulled away and Ginny knew that he had gone back into his shell again. The happy Theo who had laughed and smiled a short time earlier was lost forever.

The horse and cart was waiting for them when they walked back into the field. It was piled high with an assortment of suitcases. Badblood was heaving Archie and Millie into the back like sacks of potatoes while Antonia sat up front holding the reins. She was wearing a frilly yellow dress and red boots. She had a pink hat on her head with one of Blue's feathers sticking out of it and a green shawl covered her shoulders. Her red boots were laced up tight, and she wore white lace fingerless gloves. Her red curls bounced on her shoulders. The horse was getting uneasy, and Antonia pulled the reins back.

"Hurry up, will ya, Ginny!" she called.

Theo climbed on the cart and held out his hand to Ginny, but she turned away and climbed on board herself. She sat on top of a brown suitcase which was secured with a long red silk scarf.

Badblood twirled his moustache between his fingers and smiled to reveal his gold teeth. Then he took the reins from Antonia, and she leant her head on his shoulder.

The horse plodded along the cobbled streets of Dublin. They went past the Four Courts, along the Liffey and down Grafton Street. Badblood tipped his hat at the men and women who walked by and Antonia waved at them flamboyantly. People smiled at the curious-looking gentleman and assumed that Antonia was his wife.

Archie looked at Millie.

Ginny knew that they were communicating through thought-reading and she turned to tell Theo, but he was asleep. He looked peaceful although he was awkwardly propped up against some suitcases as there was no room to lie down on the cart. Ginny could see the apple-shaped birthmark his cheek and the dimple in the centre of his chin. She resisted the

105

urge to reach out and touch him. He had taken such good care of her ever since the night when she was robbed and left for dead on Bleeding Heart Street. Ginny wanted to believe that Theo was a good person although recent events, such as the aggressive way he treated Millie, seemed to prove otherwise.

Theo had lived a hard life. He had to fend for himself on the streets of London from a young age. The gift of being able to see how people were going to die was a terrible burden for anyone to carry. Theo never spoke about his family and Ginny guessed that they had abandoned him when they knew about his gift, just as her family had abandoned her.

Ginny's mind drifted back to the last circus show. She knew that Theo had the ability to see when and where she was going to die. She wished that they had seen everything that night, no matter how painful it was for her. Then perhaps she could do something to prevent it. Although she knew it was pointless thinking that way.

As the horse and cart trundled along the road, Ginny could not help but wonder if Badblood was taking her to the strange forest where the wicked women who had appeared in Theo's vision lived.

The bustling city streets melted away and fields dotted with weeping willow trees came into view. As they meandered along the winding country lanes, the green fields turned black. Crows circled overhead.

A family knelt in the ditch at the side of the road. A young girl was crying over the body of her dead grandmother who had a string of rosary beads wrapped around her fingers. The girl's parents bowed their heads and prayed over her. When the girl's mother saw Badblood, she ran up to the cart and pleaded with him to take their daughter with him.

"Please, sir, give her a better life. She's a good girl!"

"There is no room for another one," Badblood said. Then he hit the woman across the back with his cane and she fell to the ground.

Ginny watched the family fade into the distance like a memory. The girl's black eyes were empty and cold. She locked eyes with Ginny, who could see that the girl was starving – her ribs were visible beneath her brown dress. Ginny longed to help her, but she knew that there was nothing that she could do except hope and pray that the girl would have a quick death.

Four days later, in the evening, they reached County Wexford and settled down for the night in a village called Ferns.

Ginny overheard Antonia telling Badblood that there was a soup kitchen in Ferns, which was set up by the Quakers, to feed the people affected by the Famine. However, when they reached Ferns, they were told that the soup kitchen had shut down.

"Soup would have been nice for you, my dear

children. But it won't do you any harm to go without a hot meal for one day!" said Badblood.

Theo had to resist the urge to lash out at him as he pretended to be a caring father.

A man with black teeth and a patch over his left eye told Badblood that he should leave the children in the workhouse.

"At least they will be cared for there," he said.

Ginny did not know what would be worse – Badblood's circus or the workhouse.

They stopped beside the ruins of a castle. The lights of fires were scattered all around it. Badblood told them that the castle once belonged to Diarmuid MacMurragh, who was the King of Leinster. Then he lit a fire and they huddled around it for warmth.

"We're not staying here, are we?" Ginny asked Antonia, when Badblood's back was turned.

"Of course we are, my dear. Badblood likes to sleep beneath the stars and, on a clear night like this, if you look closely you can see the Man in the Moon."

All around them were fires. Amber flames burned bright, logs crackled and sparks flew into the smoky air. Ginny looked up to the sky. The moon seemed closer to them than usual, and it looked like a large orange in the sky.

Badblood took a small loaf of mouldy bread out of one of the cases and handed a piece of it to each of the children.

"Here, this will have to do you. Never let it said that Badblood is not a kind and generous man."

The children were so hungry that they ate every crumb. As they ate Antonia reached into her large red-velvet bag and pulled out a tablecloth. She laid it on the ground and then produced two plates, two knives and two forks, in much the same way as a magician pulls a rabbit out of a hat. Then she revealed hardboiled eggs, slices of ham and buttered bread for herself and Badblood to dine on. They washed it down with bottles of stout.

Once they had finished eating, Badblood pulled a harmonica out of his pocket, and people gathered around to listen to him play. Antonia sang a song about a place called Vinegar Hill and a man told them a story about a boy who fell in love with a ghost.

When the music finally stopped, and Badblood and Antonia had fallen asleep, Ginny turned to Theo, who was biting his fingernails.

"Where do you think they're taking us?"

"I don't know, but I have a very bad feeling about this."

Ginny looked over at Millie and Archie, who were curled up like kittens next to each other. Theo sensed Ginny's fear and put his arm around her. She moved closer to him for warmth.

"Where has the circus gone, Theo?"

"I don't know, Ginny, but as bad as it was I think

things are about to get worse."

Ginny lay back in the grass and looked up at the stars. The full moon crawled up the sky and shone down on them.

"I am going to die, Theo."

"Don't say that, Ginny." Theo pulled away from her and placed his head in his hands.

"You saw my death in that woman's eyes."

"Stop it, Ginny."

"I want to know, Theo, please."

Theo stood up and walked away.

Ginny was woken up in the early hours of the morning by the sound of Antonia's voice.

"Get on the cart now, Ginny!"

Ginny looked around and saw a group of people nearby but she couldn't see Antonia. Nor was Antonia on the cart which Badblood was hurriedly mounting.

"Theo! Wake up!"

Theo sat up immediately, hearing the alarm in her voice.

"Hurry!" Badblood shouted from the cart.

Ginny and Theo shook the two children awake.

"What's wrong, Ginny?" Millie asked.

"Nothing, Millie. We're just leaving."

As soon as the children were on board Badblood whipped the horse with his cane and they sped off along the dusty road.

Ginny looked back and at last saw Antonia. She was in the centre of the group of people. Her yellow dress was torn, her hair dishevelled. The green silk scarf that had been tied around her neck had fallen to the ground. The people were angry. A woman spat at her, and a man grabbed her by the arms and held her tight.

Ginny hated leaving her behind and started to cry.

Then Antonia shouted at the top of her lungs: *"Don't let them get you down, treasure! This world is yours for the taking!"*

Ginny turned to Badblood and placed her hand on his shoulder. "You can't leave her! Please turn back!"

"Do you want to get us all killed, girl?"

"They are hurting her."

"Antonia can take care of herself. Just shut up."

"Theo, we have to do something!" Ginny pleaded. "Please!"

"Would you listen to yourself, Ginny? She's the reason that we're in this mess."

"But Theo!"

"Why do you care so much about her?" He felt angry with Ginny. Antonia had some hold over her, and he didn't like it.

Antonia's green shawl was on the seat next to Badblood. Ginny reached over and took it. She wrapped it around her shoulders over her own blue one, then she turned away from Theo and held the

111

shawl up to her nose. It smelt of lemons and roses. She remembered the night she first met Antonia, how she had undressed behind the screen, then had given her the gold cross on the chain.

Although Ginny knew that Theo was right and Antonia had turned out bad in the end, she could not help feeling a fondness for her. She rubbed the shawl against her cheek. Then she fell asleep and dreamt of Antonia in her voluminous pink ballet tutu, with millions of sparkling pearls embroidered onto her silk bodice. Her red hair was falling in waves over her bare shoulders while she danced like a ballerina on the back of a brown horse.

Chapter nine

Inis Rua
The Tiger Moth's Death

Lightning streaked the opaque sky. Claps of thunder rumbled like a giant with a bellyache. They boarded the small green fishing boat and made their way across to the island.

The boat tumbled along the icy black waves. Archie held Millie's hair back as she got sick over the side. His riding hat blew into the water and was borne away by the waves.

Badblood spoke to the boatman in Irish. He was an old man with a long red beard. He wore a pea-green jumper with holes in the sleeves and there was a sparrow with a broken wing perched on his left shoulder. A clay pipe hung from his bottom lip and Ginny was not sure how it stayed there as the man spoke.

There was a dense fog that made it difficult for them to tell when they were near the shore. But then a tremendous mountain came into view. It split the fog like an axe. The boatman explained to them that the island was called Inis Rua and that *rua* was the word for red in Irish. Ginny couldn't understand why it was called 'Red Island' when it was covered in purple heather, but she knew better than to ask. On top of the mountain, pointing towards the clouds, was a large crucifix. It looked like it was made of wood.

Two peculiar women stood on the shore waiting for them to arrive. They were peculiar for a number of reasons. Both women had long black hair with a red streak in it. It was parted in the centre of their heads. The children had never seen women with such long hair before. It ran down their backs, over their shoulders and trailed behind them.

Ginny shuddered to see them, remembering Theo's vision of her death.

"Maud and Petulia Witcherly are waiting for us on the shore – how delightful!" Badblood exclaimed.

The Witcherly sisters wore purple dresses that were buttoned up to the neck. The only part of their bodies that could be seen was their hands and faces.

Their faces were covered in green pus-filled warts that looked ready to explode. Millie thought that the women could use the leeches that had saved her on the ship. One of the women had a mole above her left eye with three coarse red hairs protruding from it, and the other one had a silver locket around her neck with the initial "*P*" engraved on it. Ginny realised that she must be Petulia Witcherly. Her long yellow fingernails curled over at the end and Ginny wondered if they had ever been cut. Her hair trailed down her back, like the black tongue of a giant.

The wind got worse as the children scrambled onto the shore and it whispered to them "*Go back, go back!*" Archie heard it and Millie did too. But there was no going back – the boatman had already left the shore. His boat was out there wrestling with the waves. They were trapped. Thunder rattled the ground beneath their feet and a flash of lightning split a tree in half.

The Witcherly sisters led the children into a dense forest. The sky above them turned purple and then black like a bruise and a red moon crouched behind the clouds. Ginny looked at the mountain. The moon rose in the sky and turned the mountain from purple to red. She realised that was how the island got its name.

Leaves crunched beneath their feet and a beetle scurried in the undergrowth. A badger bared its teeth and ran for cover. A nettle stung Archie on the hand and a red rash appeared on his pale skin. He found a dock leaf and rubbed his hand until the pain subsided. The smell of the trees and the flowers was intoxicating. Damp, earthy smells of dandelions and roses filled the air. Millie had to concentrate hard so that she didn't shift shapes and turn into a fox.

An owl with yellow eyes the colour of the sun turned its square head towards them, hooted and looked away in disgust.

They walked deeper into the forest. Thickets and brambles stretched out towards them like bony fingers. A blackbird picked a red berry off the branch of a tree and flew back to its nest.

Ginny felt tired, her back ached and her throat was sore. She sighed with relief when the Witcherly sisters' home came into view.

The crooked chimney reached up to the sky. It spat plumes of black smoke up into the air. The lightning flashed again and four bats flew overhead. There was a gate at the front of the house. It formed the shape of a heart. A spider had spun a silver web in the centre of it. Maud Witcherly opened the creaky gate. Her long fingernails scraped off the metal.

The Witcherly sisters led the children along the path towards the front door.

A knocker shaped like a lion with a ring between its teeth reminded Ginny of the circus. She looked back to see if Badblood had noticed it but he had disappeared. A shiver ran down Ginny's spine.

The door squeaked as Petulia pushed it open.

Theo was the last to enter the house. As soon as he stepped inside Maud slammed the door shut. Then she took a set of keys off a piece of black ribbon that she wore around her neck and locked it. There were three locks on the door and each lock had a different key.

Theo looked around and noticed that someone was missing.

"Where's Badblood?"

"Miss him, do ya?" As Maud spoke, she opened her mouth.

Theo noticed that she had only two black teeth left – they jutted out from her gums like gravestones.

"I was just wondering."

"You can stop your wondering, boy, do you hear me?"

Maud pushed her fingernail into Theo's cheek and left a dent there. Her breath smelt like rotten eggs. He turned his face away and looked at Millie and Archie, who had their faces buried in Ginny's arms.

The hallway was narrow and dark and there were no windows. On one wall was a painting of the Witcherly sisters. It hung on a rusty nail. In the painting they were standing outside the house, and they looked younger than they did now. In the background were children. But they did not look like ordinary children. They all appeared to have special gifts just like Theo, Ginny, Millie and Archie. One boy had no head – another girl was flying through the air.

Opposite the painting was a mirror in a gold frame.

It had warped and the glass was mottled with black flecks.

A tiger moth sat on the edge of the mirror. Millie touched its amber-and-black wings and it flew towards her and became entangled in her hair. Millie screamed. Petulia turned towards her and clipped a clump of her hair off with her long fingernails. Then she stamped on the tiger moth. Millie flinched as Petulia lifted her foot and the moth's tiny wings stopped beating.

"Stop crying, you evil child!" Maud snapped. "Come with me."

Then she walked ahead of the children up a winding staircase.

Millie sobbed as she thought of the tiny moth. She detested herself for causing such a fuss. It was her fault that the tiger moth had died.

Halfway up the staircase there was a landing. Millie noticed a writing desk with books on it, and a glass dome containing water and a winter scene.

Petulia picked up one of the books and tucked it under her arm. Millie thought that it must be a book of spells. Archie saw it too and he gave his sister a pitiful glance.

At the top of the stairs was a room with a sloped ceiling. Inside, the children could see that it was a children's nursery. There was a dapple-grey rocking horse over by the window and a large doll's house which was painted green. Millie peered through the windows. There were miniature rooms with miniature furniture. Millie was confused; perhaps the Witcherly sisters wouldn't be too bad after all.

"This is where you'll be staying," Petulia said. As she spoke a string of saliva hung from her top lip and a decaying tooth flapped about like a kite inside her mouth.

Then she turned towards the door, with Maud by her side.

"We are hungry and thirsty," Theo said when he realised that they were being left in the room.

"You insolent boy! Do you really expect us to feed you?" Petulia roared then she slapped Theo hard across the cheek.

His apple-shaped birthmark appeared redder than ever. If it were hanging from a tree, it would have been ripe for picking.

Ginny got down on her knees.

"Please feed us! We haven't eaten in days," she begged.

"At least a glass of water." Archie's voice croaked as he spoke.

"You wicked, evil children! There is only one cure for you and that is starvation." Petulia's voice was gentler, caring almost. She bent down and stroked Ginny's face. "Can't you see that if we feed you we feed the evil that lurks inside you?"

119

"What does she mean, Archie?" Tears trickled down Millie's cheeks,

But it was too late. The Witcherly sisters were gone.

The children sat on the metal beds and listened to the door being locked from the outside and the sound of the storm as it lashed against the window.

Chapter ten

Inis Rua
The Ghost Circus

Millie sat on the cold wooden floor and played with the doll's house. There were four porcelain dolls inside the house: two boys and two girls. They were seated around an oval-shaped mahogany table. There were four elegant chairs with red-silk cushions and legs that resembled lion's claws. The table was set for a banquet with tiny gold cups and plates. A crystal chandelier hung from the ornate ceiling. Each delicate crystal looked like a fairy's tooth.

The dolls were dressed in perfectly tailored clothes. One of them wore a blue blouse and a long green skirt. This was Millie's favourite doll. She placed her at the head of the table. The doll reminded Millie of her mother who was miles away in London. Her heart ached to see her again.

Ginny looked out of the window and her sad reflection stared back at her. She hardly recognised herself. Her cheeks looked hollow – it was as though they were carved from the bough of a tree. Her eyes were as black as coal and her hair was limp. Ginny felt like she was back in the Hall of Mirrors, although what she was seeing was not an illusion.

She looked through herself and stared at an ancient oak tree that stood in the garden. Its sprawling branches reached out like fingers and a swing hung from a rope that was suspended from it. The seat had been carved from wood and was worn in the centre. Ginny thought that it must have been used a lot over the years. It swayed back and forth in the breeze, as though an unseen force was driving it. Ginny imagined an invisible girl, or perhaps a ghost, swinging on it. She pressed her face against the glass. Condensation trickled down the windowpane like small rivers. She traced the outline of the tree with her finger and watched the swing moving through the air.

Theo lay on the small metal bed and stared at the ceiling. The blankets scraped his chin. He pulled Badblood's knife out of his coat pocket and scratched each of their names into the wooden beam above his head. *Ginny, Theo, Millie, Archie*. Underneath their names, he wrote the word *HELP*. Then he placed the knife back into his pocket and turned to watch Millie playing with the dolls.

Theo had never known his mother and father, so he had no memories of home to torment him. But Archie and Millie were different. They had lived a privileged life before they were captured. They had known a mother's love and losing that could be enough to break them.

Archie sat on the floor, with his ear pressed against the door. His left knee was bent and he rested his elbow on it. He was listening out for the slightest sound. However, all that he could hear was the sound of mice scuttling around beneath the floorboards. He was hungry, they all were, but he knew better than to mention it. He looked at his red coat and his black riding boots – he knew he looked ridiculous. At the time he left home he had thought it would be a good idea to dress up like a ringmaster. Now he hated the circus. He longed to go back in time. If he could, he would go back to the exact moment that he had decided to leave home and he would stop himself.

He turned and looked at Millie. She was playing with a doll. It wore a blue blouse and green skirt. Millie brushed its hair with a tiny silver comb and held it close. Archie knew that the doll reminded her of their mother. Sometimes Millie's thoughts escaped without her knowledge. They flew through the air like a bird and entered Archie's mind. This happened when she felt pain or when she was sad. He knew how much she missed their mother – he missed her too. He

123

also knew that Millie blamed him for everything and there was nothing he could do to make it up to her.

The footsteps on the stairs startled Archie. He jumped up. Millie sensed her brother's fear and dropped the doll – it fell to the floor. She stood on the silver comb and it broke in two as she scrambled over to her brother's side. A key turned in the lock and Archie and Millie stepped back.

Petulia Witcherly stood there in a red-velvet cloak, with the letter "P" embroidered onto it with gold and silver thread. Beneath the cloak she was wearing an emerald-green ball gown which was embellished with thousands of emeralds – they illuminated the dark room. Around her neck was a red ribbon and a silver heart-shaped locket hung from it with the image of a peacock on the front. On her face, she wore a black crow-shaped carnival mask. A long yellow beak protruded from the centre of the mask which was covered in ink-black feathers.

The sound of music – an accordion and a violin – travelled up the stairs. Petulia carried a golden tray containing four green goblets and a jug of water. A slice of lemon floated on the surface. And Millie noticed four pips lying at the bottom of the jug.

"Drink this, then come outside. They are all waiting for you."

She left the golden tray on the floor and drifted out of the room, her long black hair trailing after her. There was a bad smell in the air.

Archie reached for the water.

"It's a trick," Theo said as he pulled the jug from the boy's hand. The water dripped onto the floor.

"Give it back!" Archie shouted. His lips were dry and cracked and his throat scratched.

Ginny touched Theo's arm. "We have to drink it, Theo. Without water we'll die."

Theo loosened his grip on the jug and Archie poured them all a drink.

After they had drunk the water, they stared at the open door.

"What should we do?" Archie asked.

Millie looked at Ginny, and Ginny turned to Theo.

"I know one thing," he said. "I am not staying in here any longer."

Theo walked out of the room.

Then he gasped. "You have to see this!"

The others followed him outside.

Hundreds of church candles lined the walls and flickered in the darkness. Blue lanterns containing red candles were placed on each of the wooden steps. A red-velvet carpet had been secured to the centre of the stairs and yellow rose petals formed a trail along the centre of the carpet. The sound of the accordion drifted through the air.

"It looks so beautiful," Millie said. A tear sparkled in the corner of her eye.

The smell of candlewax and smoke drifted through the air. A chandelier hung from the ceiling. Golden flames danced on white tapered candles. It reminded Millie of the chandelier in the doll's house.

At the bottom of the staircase, a crowd of people had assembled. The women wore brightly coloured wigs. One woman wore a canary-yellow dress and on her head was a pink wig. It was at least two foot tall. On top of the wig was a cuckoo. It sat in a nest made from twigs. The woman's eyelashes matched the colour of her wig and she blinked continually.

Another of the women was tall and slim. She had long blue eyelashes and a bright purple wig on her head which resembled a wedding cake.

The women smelt like honey blossom and oranges. They held harlequin masks in their dainty fingers and hid behind them whenever they wanted to whisper to each other.

Two strapping men stepped out of the shadows as the children descended. They looked like Millie and Archie's butlers, Fred and Paul. Except that they were no ordinary men. They had horses' heads. Both men were wearing long black coats and they balanced silver trays in their hands. Millie glanced down and was not one bit surprised when she saw hoofs instead of feet.

There were two envelopes on each of the silver trays with the children's names written on them beautiful gold letters. The envelopes were sealed with a red stamp that was embossed with the name *Badblood*.

Ginny carefully opened the envelope with the bone-handled letter-opener that was placed on the tray. A purple-and-green butterfly flew out of the envelope. There was an invitation inside.

1848

Night of the Blood-Red Moon

Bird Girl,

We invite you to join the carnival. It will be the most spectacular show you ever witness. All of the magical performers are Ghosts. Be with us on this Night of a Blood-Red Moon and dazzle the world forever.

Ever yours,

Badblood

Ginny walked over to a wooden writing desk and looked at a jar of black roses with sharp green thorns. Beside it a tapered gold candle was burning. She placed a corner of the invitation into the amber flame and watched as the fire devoured the ink. She held the burning page between her finger and thumb. Then she tossed it into the air and watched as it turned to dust.

The people stood back in amazement, then they clapped and cheered.

"*Bravo!*" said a voice Ginny knew only too well.

She spun around and saw Billy Beak.

"Shall we go outside, my dear? The show is about to commence."

127

Billy Beak linked Ginny's arm and they walked outside. Theo, Millie and Archie walked behind them, followed by the Witcherly sisters and the eager crowd.

The trees were decorated with blue, green and yellow ribbons. They were tied in bows and hung from the crooked branches.

Yellow-and-red birds of paradise flew in and out of the trees. Pale stars twinkled in the sky and the moon was the colour of blood. It shone down from above. Silver tufts of grass stretched up like silver daggers beneath their feet.

Ginny turned to Billy Beak. His skin shimmered under the moonlight. She put her hand up to touch him, but her fingers went straight through his body and came out the other side.

"You're a ghost!" Ginny cried, and she placed her hand over her mouth.

"We all are, dear," said the woman in the pink wig. Even the cuckoo that peeped out from the candyfloss wig shimmered.

"Ginny, look!" Theo nudged Ginny with his elbow.

There was a heart-shaped archway in the trees made from holly leaves and red berries, and a path that appeared to go on forever. A boy walked towards them. As he got closer, the children realised that he was no ordinary boy. He was the ghost of a boy. He held his head in his hands and he wore an orange waistcoat and brown trousers.

"Follow me," he instructed.

The children did as they were told.

Theo levitated. He could not help himself – his feet left the ground and he flew through the air. Millie shapeshifted into a fox. She was powerless to stop herself. Ginny could feel Blue's wings flapping inside of her.

She looked down and she could not believe her eyes. She was able to see inside her body. Her red heart thumped like the beat of a drum. Her rib bones were smooth. They were woven together to form a bird cage. Blue was inside, perched on a swing made from a piece of her rib.

The children walked through the heart-shaped archway. The ghosts of more and more children appeared from behind the trees. They stepped in front of them. Each of them had magical abilities. One boy had eyes on the back of his head, which swivelled around as he walked. Another girl with black hair had a face without any eyes, nose or mouth.

When they reached the end of the path, the enchanting music continued and then, as if by magic, Mr Moonshine appeared, playing the violin.

An almighty roar shook the leaves from the trees and Blue jumped out of Ginny's ribcage. Then in a shimmering and glittering light Antonia appeared on the back of the liger. She looked beautiful in her gold-sequinned costume.

"*Antonia!*" Ginny cried. She ran towards her and put her arms out.

But Antonia and the liger ran straight through her. Millie screamed as Ginny fell to the ground.

Then the sound of two women singing could be heard, from deep within the forest. After a moment, the Siamese Twins sauntered out. They were wearing a lace wedding dress and carried a bouquet of dandelions in their hands. They walked up to Ginny and smiled, then they drifted through the air like a memory.

Ginny looked up through the shimmering trees. A shooting star flew across the sky, in front of the blood-red moon. Then millions of tiger moths flew from the trees and covered the children from head to toe.

The circus performed until late in the night. Then, as the moon reached the highest point in the sky, they all followed Mr Moonshine. He played his violin and led them to the edge of the forest.

Then, one by one, the circus performers disappeared into the shadows of the trees and the whisper of the wind in the long grass. Billy Beak and Antonia were the last to vanish. They shimmered in the darkness. Antonia kissed Ginny on the cheek and Billy Beak waved them a fond farewell as they walked along the path that led them out of the forest and on towards their death.

Chapter eleven

Inis Rua
The Death of Magnificent Children

Petulia Witcherly tied the children's hands behind their backs with thick red rope. Then Maud placed tape over their lips so that they could not scream. The blood-red moon was at its highest point in the sky. Petulia felt excited that the Prophecy of the Blood-Red Moon was close to being fulfilled. The Witcherly sisters were Guardians of the Prophecy. It was their responsibility to see that it was properly fulfilled. They could go to their graves now knowing that the task was complete.

The Witcherly sisters led the children out of the Crooked Forest. Millie noticed an owl with yellow eyes hooting on a wooden fence. It looked as though it was saying goodbye. Ginny thought of Badblood's circus. She recalled Antonia and Billy Beak. They had been ghosts all along. She blinked away the tears. She knew that it would all be over soon. There would be no need for tears any more.

The road swung before them like the pendulum on a clock. They could hear the sound of the waves pounding against the shore. Ginny stumbled on a rock and fell to the ground. Her leg started to bleed. Petulia picked her up by her hair and told her to keep walking. In the distance, they could see the village. Stone cottages with slanted roofs emitted wispy strings of smoke from black chimneypots into the sky. There were candles in the windows.

At the foot of the mountain they walked past a cottage. It belonged to the gravedigger. Petulia was pleased with him; she thought that he had done a good job on the graveyard. He had spent months making the heart-shaped iron gates just as she had requested. People would believe that it was an ordinary graveyard – they would not know the dark secrets that it contained.

Something about the Gravedigger's Cottage caught Archie's eye. He stopped for a moment. Two names drifted through his mind as gentle as a summer's breeze. Thomas and Agatha. He did not know anyone called Thomas and Agatha and yet the names were as clear in his mind as the names of his own parents.

They walked up the mountain. Abandoned cottages with stone walls greeted them – they were dotted up the mountainside like pieces on a chessboard. A scrawny feral cat ran past with a dead rat in his mouth and Millie looked away.

Halfway up the mountain, it started to snow. They walked past a sheep's skull – a worm wriggled in its eye socket and Archie wondered how long it had been lying there and where the rest of its bones were.

As they approached the top of the mountain, they saw that a crowd of people had gathered. They appeared to be waiting for them. They were holding torches and red sparks flew into the air. The people were nothing like the ghosts from the circus. These people were very much alive. They looked old and worn, their skin weather-beaten, their faces like lines on a map. They spoke Irish in hushed voices. The women pulled shawls around their shoulders and blessed themselves as the children walked past.

A man dressed in black appeared. He held a copy of the Bible in his hand and sprinkled water on each of the children's heads. Then he spoke the words of the prophecy:

"You will sleep for one hundred years and then, on a night of a Blood-Red Moon, you will wake and wander the world for the rest of eternity."

He led them past a stone wall which had ivy trailing up it. A metal gate in the shape of a heart led them into a graveyard. There were four open graves at the back. A man with a flat cap on his head stood leaning on a shovel. He was chewing on a blade of grass and stood up straight when they walked past. He winked at Petulia Witcherly and Ginny thought that she saw her blush.

In the centre of the graveyard was a pile of wood. Broken-up pieces of furniture, tables, chairs, wardrobes and dressers were thrown together to create the largest bonfire the children had ever seen.

A man stepped forward: it was Badblood. He looked as though he was alive again. Millie thought of the first time she saw him. He twirled his moustache between his fingers and smiled to reveal his gold teeth. On his hands were a pair of black leather gloves and a top hat rested on his head.

Ginny looked at Theo and shook her head. They watched as Badbood put his hand into his pocket. Then he pulled out a silver pocket watch. Archie recognised it as his father's watch.

Badblood moved towards the children; then he looked up at the sky. He waited until the hands on the clock reached midnight and the red moon moved into position, then he dangled the silver pocket watch before Archie's eyes.

"Here you go, young man. I do believe that this belongs to you," he said and placed the watch into the pocket of Archie's red coat.

Then he led the children to four mahogany thrones that had suddenly appeared in a line next to the bonfire. Each throne was fitted with a red silk cushion.

The legs were carved in the shape of lions' claws. He instructed them to sit down. Then he tied each of them into the chairs with silken ropes.

Maud Witcherly stepped forward, brandishing a torch. Her face looked vile. Her pus-filled warts and bent nose appeared worse under the orange light. She lit the bonfire. Pieces of wood began to crackle and burn. The flames danced higher and higher. Tables and chairs were all devoured by the ravenous fire. Then the flames changed colour from orange to blood-red and they formed the shape of a heart.

In the centre of the heart, a group of witches wearing red-velvet robes stood around a cauldron. The children recognised the oldest witch: she was the old woman with the bulging eyeballs from the circus. Her eyeballs rolled out, then they transformed into silver stars and floated up into the sky. Behind the witches a long wooden table was set for a banquet. There were golden goblets encrusted with emeralds and in the centre of the table was a roast pig on a gold plate with an apple in its mouth. Two thrones resembling the ones that the children were tied to sat at opposite ends of the table. The letters "M" and "P" had been carved into them.

One of the witches, with long golden hair and teeth shaped like daggers, read a spell from a leather-bound book: *"On this, the night when the Prophecy of the Blood-Red Moon will at last be fulfilled, come and join us, sisters!"*

Then she beckoned the Witcherly sisters with a hooked finger.

Maud and Petulia Witcherly stepped into the centre of the blood-red heart, and the witches cackled as the flames engulfed them. As the Witcherly sisters disappeared from sight, the children watched the old eyeless witch from the circus, her face twisted in a grotesque way until it took the form of the face of a wild beast, a cross between a bear and a lion. Then she howled at the blood-red moon as the angry fire covered her like a cloak.

Sweat trickled down Millie's face. She tried to escape, but it was no use. The fire was getting closer to them. The heat was unbearable.

Ginny looked into the amber flames, and she saw a beautiful woman dressed in a pink tutu and a silk bodice tied together with blue ribbon, riding on the back of an elephant. There was also a beautiful woman from Siam.

An audience appeared and a circus ring. A man with a face shaped like the moon was playing a violin and another man with a black beard held a jar containing leeches. Millie looked towards Archie.

They were blinded by the light of the fire. They shut their eyes and when they opened them again they were inside the flames in a golden halo of light. They discovered that they were just in time for the circus show to begin.

PART TWO

1948

The Little Boy Found

The little boy lost in the lonely fen,
 Led by the wand'ring light,
 Began to cry, but God ever nigh,
 Appeared like his father in white.

He kissed the child and by the hand led
 And to his mother brought,
Who in sorrow pale, thro' the lonely dale
 Her little weeping boy sought.

William Blake – Songs of Innocence – 1789

Chapter twelve

Inis Rua
The Scream from the Graveyard

Thomas and Agatha Brennan lived in Gravedigger's Cottage. Although the gravedigger had been long since gone, his shovel remained propped outside the door of the cottage as a constant reminder of the job that he had performed there years ago.

The cottage was shaped like a tombstone. Ivy trailed up the damp walls and a thatched roof provided a home for the sparrows and crows that nested there. Gravedigger's Cottage jutted out of the foot of the mountain like a big toe; it had been abandoned for years before the Brennans moved there, as the islanders believed that the cottage was haunted.

Thomas and Agatha were sitting by the fireside on a cold winter night. They were listening to the sound of the waves as they crashed against the jagged rocks that lined the shore. Thomas was wearing brown woollen trousers and a black shirt. His brown hair was turning grey at the temples, and deep lines hung around his lips like commas. A clay pipe hung from his bottom lip and sent occasional puffs of smoke up into the air. He watched the amber flames dance from the fire and cast shadows across the bare floorboards. The shadows formed strange shapes in the darkness. He thought he saw a tiger and then a bear.

Agatha was sewing when the sound of a child's scream pierced the silence. It sent a shiver down her spine and caused her to prick her finger on the needle. Bright red blood stained the white lace cloth that she held between her finger and thumb.

"There it is again, Agatha – did you hear it this time?"

Agatha looked at her husband. He was not one to scare easily. She picked up her sewing and looked away from him as she spoke because she didn't want him to see that she too was scared. Instead, she concentrated on the red thread as it created the pattern of a flower on the small square handkerchief.

"It must be the storm, Thomas. A bad night can play tricks on the mind."

"No, Agatha, it is not the storm. I heard the sound of a child screaming. It came from the mountain."

Thomas walked across the kitchen floor and peered out of the small square window. A dung-beetle climbed onto the windowsill as a blood-red moon shone down on the island like a torch.

Thomas could see the silhouette of the large wooden cross that had been placed on top of the mountain after the Famine, to mark the graves of the people buried there. According to the Island Keepers, the cross kept intruders away and showed outsiders that people living on Inis Rua were God-fearing people.

He thought the islanders were primitive folk. They developed strange customs and beliefs because they were cut off from the outside world by the sea that surrounded their rugged shores.

However, on this particular night with the blood-red moon high in the sky, as he sat at the kitchen table and put his boots on, with the sound of the wind howling outside his door and the screams of the child getting louder, Thomas wondered if the islanders' superstitions were justified after all, and he made a promise to himself never to mock them again. Although he would never tell Agatha this or she would call him a foolish old man.

Agatha put her sewing down on the table. Her fingers had grown tired, and her eyesight wasn't as it used to be. She recalled how she had made her wedding dress twenty years earlier. She had worked all through the night. Each stitch fell into place as she made the ivory-lace dress that she later used to make a christening gown for her son Walter.

Her fingers were nimble then and her eyes bright. She let out a heavy sigh as she thought of Walter and then she stood up and cleared away the blue-and-white-striped dinner plates from the table. The plates were the last of the wedding gifts to remain. Her mother had given them to her; they had been in her family for generations. Next to Thomas's plate was a chipped mug containing cold tea. A brown ring stained the inside of the cup.

Thomas took a mouthful of tea then he stood up and put on his heavy brown coat that hung on a metal hook on the back of the kitchen door. As he fastened the buttons on his coat, Agatha noticed how it had grown smaller on him. He had started to put on weight recently. She knew that it was her fault – she had been giving him extra portions. She still cooked enough for three people even though there were just the two of them now.

Thomas looked at his wife. Her face appeared flushed from the heat of the fire and her eyes looked black under the lamplight although they were a deep chocolate brown, speckled with hints of green. Her long blonde hair had started to turn grey and was tied up into a bun with a blue-velvet ribbon. Thomas noticed that a stray hair had come loose – it was stuck to her lip. He gently reached out and removed the hair.

Agatha smiled, to reveal an almost perfect set of

teeth. She had a slight gap in the centre which was the sign of a great singer, or at least that is what her father had told her before he left for the war when she was a child.

When she thought of her father, it was those words that she remembered most. Agatha wore a full calf-length navy skirt and a white linen blouse with long full cuffed sleeves. Around her neck hung a silver locket which contained a lock of Walter's hair. Agatha was wearing her best clothes as it was Sunday. She would have liked to dress this way every day of the week although she knew that the local people would think her strange. Your best clothes were only to be worn on a Sunday.

"You can't go out in that storm, Thomas – you'll catch your death of cold."

"Stop your fussing, Aggie – I won't be long. Maybe a lamb has got stranded on top of the mountain and needs rescuing."

Agatha looked at her husband. They both knew it wasn't a lamb making such a frightening noise. Agatha had heard stories of fairies that had tricked people out of their homes at night. Thomas sensed her fear and leaned over and kissed her on the head.

"I will be back before you know it."

And before his wife had a chance to open her mouth to protest further, Thomas was gone out of the cottage and into the mouth of the storm. Agatha locked the door after him, as she did not feel safe. She had the strange feeling that someone was watching her. She looked out of the window and watched Thomas until she could see him no more. A knot twisted in her stomach. She could not bear for anything to happen to Thomas. How could she live without him? She would be left alone.

Agatha knew that she should have grandchildren to care for by now, like her sister Sarah. However, that would never happen. She felt jealous when Sarah wrote to tell her about her granddaughter Alice taking her first steps. Agatha hated herself for feeling this way but could not help it and she wished with all her heart that she hadn't moved to the strange island. It felt as though they were living on the edge of the world.

The islanders saw her as an outsider; they did not trust her with her strange English accent. Agatha missed Yorkshire and the workers' cottages beside the cotton mill where she had lived for so long. But most of all she missed her son Walter who had died during the Second World War. At times, Agatha felt angry at Thomas. She could not understand why he thought that taking her away from her friends and family would help her to deal with her grief, although she knew that her husband was trying to help her. His distant ancestors had come from Inis Rua and, although he had no family living there now, Agatha knew that Thomas had truly believed a fresh start would do them both good.

A wedge had grown between them over the last few months. Agatha wished with all her heart that Walter was still alive and was sitting with her by the fireside at their home back in England.

Her eye fell on one of two photographs which sat in silver frames on the wooden dresser beside a clock and an old Bible that had belonged to her mother. Agatha picked up the photograph and looked at the picture of her son. He looked handsome in his uniform. Agatha's heart was heavy with grief. She had lost her only son and there was nothing she could do to get him back.

As she walked into her bedroom, the rain was beating against the window pane. It was a small bedroom with a large double bed and a chest of drawers. Agatha's pet cat Stan was stretched out on a small frayed rug beside the bed. He was purring gently. When Walter was a baby the rug had been green but it had faded to a putty-grey colour over the years. Agatha bent down and stroked the black cat's fur. It dug its claws into the rug. There were times when she felt as though Stan was the only creature left in the world who understood her.

Agatha lay down on the bed which sighed under the weight of her. Then she sobbed into her pillow. She cried harder than she had ever cried before as the realisation hit her once more that she would never see Walter again.

Thomas walked up the mountain. He had shoved his hands into his pockets and pulled the collar of his coat up around his neck as the cold rain stung his face. He walked past a donkey who was chewing on a clump of yellow grass that circled a rock. The sound of the child screaming got louder and louder with each step that Thomas took.

His heart was beating like a drum in his chest. He had heard the ghost stories, and he tried to put them out of his mind as he walked towards the graveyard. The yellow grass rubbed against his legs. He could feel the sharp rocks beneath his feet and he had to walk slowly so that he didn't fall.

When he reached the four walls that surrounded the graveyard, he looked back to see how far he had come. He could see smoke billowing from the houses in the villages and lights illuminating windows and he longed to be back home sitting in front of the fire, safe and warm with Agatha by his side.

Ivy trailed up the heart-shaped metal gates that marked the entrance to the graveyard. Thomas tugged at the bolt. The gate had rusted over the years, and the bolt squeaked in resistance as he prised it open. He caught his finger on a sharp piece of metal, and a poppy-coloured bruise appeared on his skin.

Once inside the graveyard the red moon illuminated the graves that jutted out of the grass like the crooked teeth in the mouth of a giant.

The screaming came from deep inside the graveyard. Thomas followed the shrill sound along the overgrown path to a grave at the back. The wind had eased off, and a translucent mist descended, which made it difficult for him to see where he was going.

Then he noticed something moving between the headstones. At first he thought that it was a fox or a wolf as it moved swiftly, darting in and out of the shadows, but no, it was too big to be an animal. Thomas followed it until it came to halt. It appeared to be clinging to something. Thomas rubbed his eyes as he could not believe what he was seeing. There was a boy who appeared to be no more than twelve years old clinging to a headstone.

The boy was not adequately dressed for a storm. He wore a red riding coat with tails and white breeches and on his feet he wore knee-high riding boots. He was muddy from head to foot.

Thomas stood and waited for the boy to make the first move.

Chapter thirteen

Ghosts Appear

Thomas heard the rustling of leaves and the snap of a branch. He looked around and saw a red fox with green eyes staring at him. The animal startled Thomas. It was the most beautiful fox he had ever seen. It began to search for berries in the undergrowth, the tip of its red tail appearing silver in the moonlight, a shiny black nose sniffing at the ground.

Then the boy ran as fast as he could along the overgrown path, past the headstones and out of the graveyard. Thomas found it hard to keep up with him. He was not as young as he used to be; his bones creaked and his heart thumped in his chest. He had to stop to catch his breath. Agatha's instinct was right: there was something very strange, even magical at work. Thomas wondered if there was a fairy fort on the mountain somewhere. He leant against the trunk of a mountain ash and listened to the wind as it lashed its leaves. An owl was perched on the graveyard wall and it watched Thomas with piercing yellow eyes. A field mouse was trapped beneath the owl's sharp talons – it swivelled its head around and looked towards the moon as if begging it for help. The owl ruffled its dense grey feathers as the mouse wriggled its tail like a worm in the darkness.

Thomas watched the bird and noticed that it was looking at something. It was the boy. He was sitting hunched over on a large oval-shaped rock that was covered with moss. He held something shiny in his hands. Thomas thought it might be a pocket watch but with the distance between them it was hard to tell.

"Hey, boy!"

The boy turned his head but did not stand up. It was as though he was mimicking the owl. Thomas walked towards him. He had to steady himself when on closer inspection he realised that the boy resembled his dead son Walter. He had the same head of blonde hair and green eyes flecked with hints of grey. The only difference was the skin colour – this boy's skin was paler than Walter's and his hollow eyes had sunk into his skull.

Despite his well-tailored appearance, the boy looked frail. His shoulder bones protruded through his clothes and his skin looked ghastly against the fabric of his red coat. Thomas stepped closer to the boy and saw that it was a pocket watch in his hand. It looked as though it belonged to the Victorian era. It hung from a chain and small black hands pointed to Roman numerals. When the boy saw Thomas looking at it, he put it into his pocket.

"What are doing out on a night like this?" Thomas asked.

The boy did not answer. He laughed instead. There was something about the boy that unnerved Thomas although he could not tell what it was. Maybe it was just the way he had arrived on a night of the blood-red moon or maybe it was how he was dressed in this storm. However, deep down Thomas knew that it was because the boy resembled Walter.

While Thomas was deep in thought, considering all these things, the boy stood up and took hold of his hand. Thomas could not hide his amazement as he looked down at the boy. His hand was cold and small. The wind started to howl again and Thomas did the only thing that he could think of doing: he bent and pulled the boy onto his back. Then he carried him down the mountainside and on towards Gravedigger's Cottage. The boy was as light as a feather. He dug his black boots into Thomas's ribs and clung to his neck with his arms.

Smoke rose from the chimney and a candle flickered in the window.

Agatha was putting more logs on the fire when Thomas knocked on the door.

She didn't open the door immediately.

"Agatha! Let us in!"

Agatha glanced over at the clock. It was past midnight and she hoped that whoever Thomas had with him would not stay too long.

She glanced at herself in the mirror. The blue-velvet ribbon had come loose and hung down her back. She secured her hair into place with a hairclip, then she smoothed the creases out of her skirt with the back of her hand.

"Let me in, will you, woman! We're freezing out here!"

With a weary sigh Agatha lifted the latch and stood back as Thomas walked in.

At first Agatha didn't see the boy on his back. But when she turned around after shutting the door she noticed the bright red coat, the pointy black boots and the head of blonde hair.

"*Walter!*" she cried as she helped the boy to get down.

Her head started to spin as she studied the boy's face and realised that she was mistaken. The boy wasn't her son – how could he be? Her son was dead.

Stan, the cat, stalked into the kitchen. He walked between Agatha's legs and brushed his slender body against her. When he noticed the strange boy, he hissed at him and arched his back until his fur stood on end – then he ran out of the room.

"Hello."

The small voice came as a shock to both Thomas and Agatha, who looked at each other and smiled.

"My goodness, Thomas. Where on earth did you find him?"

"He was in the graveyard."

"On his own, on a night like this? What kind of a mother –"

"Agatha, not now."

"Yes, of course, I'm sorry."

She looked straight into the boy's green eyes, which were just like Walter's, then she held his hand.

"What's your name?"

"Archibald Luxbridge, but you can call me Archie."

The boy's voice sounded hoarse – no doubt from the screaming. His English accent was familiar to Thomas and Agatha and confirmed what they already suspected: the boy wasn't local.

"What an unusual name! Would you like something to eat, Archie?" Agatha tried to stay calm, although her hands trembled like a leaf in the wind as she walked over to the wooden dresser and took down a bowl and a cup.

"Yes, please, I haven't eaten in one hundred years."

Thomas laughed at the strange boy and rubbed his head fondly as he had done with Walter when he was a boy. His heart ached as he watched Agatha take care of him as if he were her son. She heated some beef stew that was left over from dinner then she ladled it into the small brown bowl. A trail of steam drifted up into the air.

Agatha sat opposite Archie and watched as he ate his meal. It was as though he was made of gold, she was so enthralled with him.

Next she undressed him and wrapped him in a blanket. His clothes were soaked and muddy so she washed them and put them to dry in front of the fire. His undergarments looked as though they came from another era. They consisted of a red all-in-one suit which was made of calico. Agatha knew that calico had been a popular fabric in Victorian times, but it had not been used to make clothes for as long as Agatha could remember.

She then put the old tin bath in front of the fire and filled it with hot water. She helped him into it and washed him all over. She rubbed soap in between his fingers and toes and washed behind his ears. She could not believe how dirty he was. Archie wriggled around like a fish and splashed water onto the floor while Agatha scrubbed him until he almost shone. A layer of dirt sat at the bottom of the bath.

Agatha lifted him from the tin bathtub and dried him with a large green towel in front of the fire. Then she dressed him in a pair of Walter's old blue-and-white striped pyjamas. It took her breath away to see him dressed in Walter's clothes.

Agatha showed Archie to the small bedroom that once was Walter's and she sang a lullaby that she used to sing to her son as he fell asleep. After a few minutes, she kissed the boy on the cheek and left the room, shutting the door gently behind her so that she wouldn't wake him.

Agatha was surprised to find that Thomas was still up. He was sitting by the fire watching the last of the flames flicker and die.

"Is the boy asleep?"

"Yes. Don't you wake him, Thomas Brennan."

"I won't."

"Why are you staring at me?"

"It's just . . ."

"What?"

"Well, it's just that I haven't seen you smile in such a long time that I had almost forgotten how pretty you are."

"You are a foolish man, Thomas Brennan. I always said that, a foolish old man."

Then there was a knock on the front door.

"Who on earth is calling at this time of night? They had better not wake Archie."

"Well, there is only one way to find out, Aggie."

Thomas walked over towards the door.

"Wait, Thomas! It's late – it might not be safe to

open the door."

"Stop worrying, Aggie. It might be someone out looking for the lad."

Agatha lowered her head in despair. Although she knew that the boy could not stay with them, she had enjoyed being his mother if only for a short time.

Thomas opened the door slowly so that a shard of light from the moon peered in and shone and slithered across the floor.

"Who is it, Thomas?"

Thomas stepped outside and looked all around.

"That's strange. I was sure that I heard a knock."

Agatha came to the door and looked out but all she could see was the branches of the oak tree swaying in the wind.

"Come inside and lock the door!" she said.

Before Agatha went to bed, she walked into the small bedroom to check on Archie. She felt his head – it was ice-cold and a dark-blue vein throbbed in his neck. Agatha reached out and touched it.

Archie looked small on the wooden bed. A large wardrobe loomed over him and there was a little cast-iron fireplace. Above this, a heart-shaped mirror hung on a bent nail.

Agatha thought that the room smelt damp as it hadn't been used for a long time, so she went out to the kitchen and returned moments later with a basket of turf. Then she went out again and brought back some straw and a bundle of sticks in her arms. She knelt down and lit the fire, using the straw as kindling. The sound of the wind whistled down the chimney as the fire crackled and for the second time that night Agatha felt as though she was being watched. She glanced over at Archie but he was fast asleep. She went back into the kitchen and collected his still-damp clothes. First putting a small fireguard in front of the fire in the bedroom, she carefully hung the clothes on a chair in front of it. She touched his red coat. The fabric looked expensive and Agatha began to wonder where Archie's parents were.

The sound of footsteps outside alerted Agatha to danger. It was as though someone was running around outside the cottage. Moments later the sound of the footsteps came from above her head. As Agatha looked up at the ceiling, a lump of plaster came loose and fell to the floor. She placed her hand over her mouth to prevent herself from screaming as she realised that there was someone or something on the roof.

She ran towards the small window at the far side of the room. At first she couldn't see anything apart from her reflection staring back and she hardly recognised herself. Then moments later the face of a young girl appeared.

Agatha screamed then stepped back and nearly fell onto Archie's bed.

The girl had pale skin with dark-blue veins visible

below the surface. Dark rings sat like half-moons under her eyes which flashed with anger as she began to pound on the window with her small fists. Agatha was petrified and for a moment she thought that the girl was going to come through the glass. But it was her resemblance to Archie that frightened Agatha the most. She wondered if this girl could be Archie's sister or even his twin.

Agatha turned to look at Archie's bed but he had vanished. The blankets that he had been sleeping on sat in a crumpled heap on the floor and his clothes were gone. Walter's pyjamas were thrown on the floor. Agatha screamed again, louder this time. Her head was sore and she felt sick.

"What in the name of God?"

Thomas bounded into the room wearing a pair of grey long johns and a pair of green woollen bed socks that Agatha had knitted for him. There was a hole in one of the socks and his big toe stuck out. His hair stood on top of his head in tufts, and his eyelids were heavy with sleep. At any other time, Thomas's appearance might have caused Agatha to laugh but on this occasion all she could do was cry.

"It's Archie! He's gone – and there's a girl!"

"What do you mean? Agatha, come back!"

But Agatha did not hear him as she ran out of the cottage. The wind rattled the trees and danced around her ankles but she did not feel it. All she wanted was

Archie. She had lost one son and she was determined not to lose another. She ran up the side of the mountain. The rain ran down the back of her neck and blinded her eyes.

"*Archie, where are you?*" she shouted but there was no reply.

When she felt a hand on her arm she thought that it was Archie but, when she turned around, she saw Thomas standing there. He had pulled on a pair of boots and his coat before coming outside.

"*Shhhhhh*, Aggie, it's all right. Come on, let's go home."

"We can't leave them out here."

"I will go out and look for them in the morning."

"But anything could happen to them – the Island Keepers could kill them."

"Come on. Let's get you home."

Thomas and Agatha walked down the mountainside together. It was the first time that Agatha had allowed Thomas to place his arm around her since Walter had died and Thomas was glad that he was able to comfort his wife.

Agatha lay awake for most of the night. She stared at the blood-red moon which she could see outside her bedroom window. Eventually, she fell asleep. Then she dreamt of Walter, Archie and the girl. They were holding hands and dancing around in a circle laughing. Their laughter made her feel happy.

Thomas watched the smile appear on Agatha's lips as she slept. He could not explain what had occurred that night. However, he did know that something wasn't right: children don't just appear in graveyards during storms.

When he drifted off to sleep he was unaware that Archie and his sister Millie were standing at the foot of his bed.

Agatha woke up in the middle of the night when she heard a loud noise above her head. She looked up and saw Millie climbing across the ceiling like a spider. She was on her hands and knees, scurrying from one side of the room to the other. Her brown hair hung down and her nails scratched at the plaster.

Archie was standing at the window tracing the curve of the moon with his finger. Agatha was terrified. She lay as still as she could in the darkness. She did not understand what was happening, although she did know that things would never be the same again on the island of Inis Rua.

Chapter Fourteen

Footsteps on the Roof

Agatha felt as though she had just drifted off to sleep when morning crept into her room like a thief. She rubbed her red-rimmed eyes – they stung with tiredness and her head ached. She yawned and let out a loud sigh.

Then she remembered the two children who had appeared during the night. She looked up at the ceiling. The paint was chipped, and there were scratch-marks down the front of the wardrobe. On the wall over her bed should be a painting of a girl in a blue dress. It was hanging there when they moved into the cottage. Agatha scarcely noticed it any more. But it was gone. There was a patch on the wall that was whiter than any other part. That was where the painting had hung.

Agatha thought of the previous night.

The moon had cast a red glow on Archie's face, and his pale skin had shimmered in the darkness. Agatha had lain in her bed afraid to move while Thomas slept soundly beside her. She had thought about Walter and tried to remember what he looked like when he was Archie's age, but all she could see was Archie's face. She sobbed into her pillow as the thought of forgetting her only child was unbearable. The girl had felt her pain, and had knelt down beside her. Then she had brushed the tears from Agatha's eyes with her hair.

Now Agatha feared that she was losing her mind. She jumped up and ran out of the room. Perhaps it had all been a dream, she thought – the screaming from the graveyard and the appearance of the children.

She noticed that the door to Walter's bedroom was slightly open. She took a deep breath and pushed the door open. Archie was fast asleep in the small wooden bed. Walter's pyjamas were still there in a heap on the floor. Archie's red coat lay across the end of the bed. Agatha noticed the painting propped up on the dressing table. The girl was nowhere to be seen. Agatha walked over to Archie and pulled the pale blue woollen blanket around his shoulders as she had done for Walter when he was a boy and he turned over to face the wall. She noticed a silver chain wound around his fingers, like a piece of string. She touched her neck and gasped as she realised that her locket had gone. She opened his hand, and the locket fell to the floor. She picked it up and fastened it around her neck.

She walked over to the window and looked outside. It had been raining all night long, and condensation caused water to trickle down the inside of the window pane. Agatha breathed onto the glass and the word *CIRCUS* appeared.

Agatha saw something moving in the long grass. It was a beautiful fox, with bright green eyes. She had never seen one so close to the cottage before. It stared at Agatha and then hid behind the oak tree.

Agatha walked out of the bedroom and down the hallway into the kitchen. A bowl of steaming water sat by the sink. Thomas had been shaving and a small blood-stained piece of paper was stuck to his chin, which told Agatha that he had nicked himself with the razor. He was dressed in his black suit, his best one that he wore to funerals. Agatha felt cold. Thomas had just lit the fire and it would be a while before the room heated up. She walked over to the window and stared up at the mountain; she knew that it held the answers to the children's appearance. She looked for the fox but it was nowhere to be seen.

Then she turned to her face towards Thomas, who looked so much older than his fifty years.

"Where did the children come from, Thomas?"

Thomas raised his eyebrows and looked at his wife. "I don't know, but I intend to find out."

"You don't think it's . . ."

"What, Aggie?"

"Well, magic or the fairies, do you?"

"Don't talk nonsense, Aggie. You of all people."

"Children don't just appear in the middle of the night, Thomas."

"There has to be a logical explanation."

"But the footsteps . . ."

"What footsteps?"

Thomas sounded angry although Agatha knew that it was just his way of dealing with things. He did not like what was happening any more than she did.

"I heard footsteps on the roof last night."

"On the roof?"

"I know it sounds –"

"I will tell you what it sounds like, Aggie."

Thomas paced up and down the kitchen floor. Agatha noticed that his trousers were creased, and the cuff of his shirt had a small tea-stain on it.

"It sounds as though someone is playing a trick on us," he said.

"A trick?"

"Yes, a trick." He pointed his finger to the front door. "Someone on this island doesn't like us. They're making fun of us, Aggie."

"I don't think it has anything to do with the islanders, Thomas."

"I am going to the village to sort this out."

"Thomas, you can't."

"Well, Agatha, do you have any better ideas?"

Thomas had not got so agitated since Walter died, and Agatha thought that he might scare Archie away, and that was the last thing she wanted to happen. She knew that she needed to calm him down.

"Sit down and I'll make some breakfast."

Thomas did as he was told. He took his jacket off and loosened his shirt collar.

Agatha put the kettle on to boil and began to make some porridge.

She could not deny that the people on the island hadn't been friendly towards them. There had been occasions when women had crossed the street to avoid her. Thomas told her that it was her imagination but Agatha knew different. They had strange customs and rituals. But that didn't explain where the children had come from.

"The children aren't from here, Thomas."

"I know, Aggie, but where did they come from? We live on an island."

"You found the boy in the graveyard, didn't you?"

"Yes."

"He was on his own, Thomas."

"I know."

"No one in their right mind would leave a child in a graveyard on top of a mountain during a storm."

"No, I mean yes, Aggie, you're right."

"Maybe there was a shipwreck."

Agatha wondered why she hadn't thought of this before. There had been many ships wrecked on the island over the years – perhaps the children had been washed up on the shore. She sat down beside her husband and took his hand. She noticed that his eyes were glistening and his bottom lip trembled.

"The boy looks like Walter, Aggie. I thought he had come back from the dead." He lowered his head as he didn't want Agatha to see him cry.

Agatha hated to see him upset. The appearance of the children had scared him. She knew what she had to do. She needed to be left alone with Archie. She felt that the boy might open up to her if Thomas wasn't there.

She quickly set a bowl of porridge in front of Thomas and made the tea.

Then, as she poured the tea, she said: "You know, you're right, Thomas. You need to go down to the village and see if you can find out what's going on. I'll stay here until the boy wakes up." She smiled at her husband – she didn't want him to see that she too was frightened.

As soon as Thomas left, Agatha heard Archie shuffling around in the bedroom. Her heart skipped a beat. It was like Walter was alive again. She walked over to the stove and heated up the porridge. Then she took the pot off the stove and sat at the table and waited for him.

Archie walked into the kitchen. He looked paler and smaller in the daylight. He smelt strange despite the fact that she had thoroughly bathed him the night before. He smelt like clay and lemon-drop sweets, and there was a hint of something else – medicine maybe.

"Good morning, Archie."

"Good morning."

"Sit down. I have some porridge for you."

Archie did as he was told. He watched Agatha walking around the small kitchen. She was wearing a long white lace nightdress and her two white feet padded across the kitchen floor. The air was stale and Archie could smell smoke from the fire. His sense of smell was heightened as he had not used it in so long. As Agatha filled his bowl with porridge, Archie noticed the silver locket that hung around her neck. He remembered taking it from her while she slept. Agatha smelt like lavender soap and Archie liked her. She reminded him of his first nursemaid Kitty. She was always so kind to him.

Archie had never been in such a small cottage before. He thought that Thomas and Agatha must be poor. It was so quiet he could hear the clock ticking on the mantelpiece. He wondered where Agatha's children were. His mother had told him that all poor people had large families. Then he noticed two photographs on the dresser. The first was of a boy sitting on a doorstep beside two glass milk bottles – he had a woman's purse in his hand and he could not have been more than two years old. The second looked like the same boy but he was much older this time and he was wearing a uniform. Archie presumed that the boy in the photographs was Agatha's son.

"Where am I?" he asked. It hurt when he spoke, so he had to whisper.

"You are on an island called Inis Rua."

"An island?"

"Yes."

Suddenly a terrible image flashed through his mind. He was with Millie and two other children. They were on top of a mountain, and it was dark. A crowd of people had gathered around them. They were brandishing torches and chanting. A man was dragging something across the ground. Archie remembered feeling scared. Millie was crying and clinging to him – her dress was torn. He began to wonder if Agatha was one of those people.

His head hurt as he looked at the photograph of the small boy on the dresser. It was in a silver frame with a dove on it. The frame began to shake violently.

Agatha looked over at it. She thought that the bird was about to take flight. She stood still and covered her mouth with her hand. The wooden spoon in her hand slipped through her fingers and it and a lump of porridge landed on the floor.

Archie could not take his eyes off the photograph

and the more he looked at it the more the frame shook, until eventually it fell from the dresser and smashed on the floor. A sharp pain shot through Archie's temple, and he put his hands up to his head.

Agatha rushed over to the photograph on the floor and carefully picked up each shard of glass and placed them on the dresser. Her hands trembled as she touched her son's face. Then she turned to Archie.

"Why did you do that?" she cried.

She walked away from the table and moved towards the door of the cottage, with the photograph held to her heart.

"Where did you come from, Archie? Tell me!" Her high-pitched scream sounded like a bird caught in a trap. She hardly ever raised her voice. Even when Walter did something to anger her, she was always calm. But this was different. There was magic of some sort involved, and she sensed that she was in danger.

Archie stood up. He felt weak and stumbled across the room towards Agatha, who caught him in her arms. His skin was so cold. She helped him over to a chair in front of the fire and he sat down.

Then she went and stood by the window with her arms folded across her chest. She waited for Archie to speak.

"Who is the boy?"

"He is my son – Walter."

"Where is he now?"

"He's dead. Now that's enough questions."

Agatha had calmed down and was beginning to think that she was overreacting. Perhaps a draught caused the frame to fall. How could Archie have caused it to happen when he was sitting across the room?

"I am dead."

"I'm sorry, Archie, what did you say?"

"I said I am dead like Walter."

"Archie, you must not say that."

Agatha suddenly became concerned for the boy. She thought that perhaps he had hit his head, and maybe he was suffering from a concussion. Yes, she thought to herself, a concussion would explain his confused state. He must have banged his head. She felt annoyed at herself for not realising this earlier. She bit her lip and walked over to him, then placed her hand on his forehead. It felt as cold as marble and a small vein throbbed in his neck.

"Maybe you should go back to bed and lie down. When Thomas gets home I'll ask him to call Doctor Foley."

An image entered Archie's mind. It felt as though he were dreaming but he was wide awake. This time he was in a dark room and the rain was beating against the window pane. He was lying on a bed in a room like a nursery. There were other children too, on the other beds. A woman with long black hair entered the room. She was wearing a red-velvet cloak and a carnival mask, and she carried a golden tray in her hands.

Then another image appeared, the image of a circus. Archie could see a man with the face of an elephant and a woman with two heads. There was another man with a black pointy moustache. The name *Badblood* drifted through Archie's mind and he felt a strange kind of sickness come over him as if he were on a boat.

Then as suddenly as the images appeared in his mind, they disappeared and Archie was aware that he was in the cottage with Agatha.

Archie looked into Agatha's eyes, and he saw kindness there. He felt that he could trust her with his story. As the morning drifted into the afternoon, Archie told Agatha what he remembered about the island of Inis Rua and the people who had lived there one hundred years earlier.

Chapter Fifteen

The Blood-Red Moon Prophecy

The blood-red moon shone down on Inis Rua for two nights following the arrival of Archie.

The islanders were not allowed to go out after dark if there was a blood-red moon in the sky. The prophecy said that strange creatures roamed the island on the night of a blood-red moon, in search of souls. The Island Keepers patrolled the island and anyone who disobeyed the curfew was killed.

Rua Power did not believe in ghosts or red-moon prophecies. He was the only teenager living on the island and he hated it. All his friends had gone and found work on the mainland, and his brother Jacob was working as a fisherman there. Rua had begged Jacob to take him with him, but his mother insisted that it wasn't time for Rua to leave the island.

"I am fifteen years old, Mam."

"I said no, Rua."

"All my friends are gone, even Jacob."

"Jacob is older than you. Your time will come."

Rua's mother Mona had lived on the island all her life. She was a plain-looking woman in her early forties with limp brown hair. Frown lines converged in the centre of her forehead which gave her the appearance of always being in a bad mood. Her eyes were grey and crow's feet tugged at the skin around her eyelids. Her cheeks were red and chapped and it looked as though her skin had been scrubbed with a wire brush.

Mona had married when she was eighteen years old, as this was the custom on Inis Rua. By the time she was twenty-five she had four children. Jacob was the eldest, followed by Rua, and then there were twin girls Ruth and Naomi, who looked like miniature versions of their mother. Mona knew that it was time to let Rua go – he was fifteen, after all – but she could not bear to part with him.

Rua's father Ezekiel Power was a preacher and the leader of the Island Keepers. He owned the book that contained the Blood-Red Moon Prophecy, which had been handed down to him from his father. Ezekiel expected Rua to follow in his footsteps, to lead the Island Keepers and to protect the islanders from evil, but Rua wanted no part in it.

"Where are you going, Rua?" Mona asked when he stood up from the table and put on his green coat.

The islanders were ordered to wear certain colour clothes that corresponded with the season of the year. As it was winter, they had to wear green. Anyone who disobeyed the rules was punished. The last person to disobey the island's rules was Pádraig, a farmer from the far side of the island. He wore a green hat in springtime. As punishment, he had to wear a heavy metal chain around his waist. It was fastened with a padlock and weighted down with rocks. Ezekiel held the key and he did not open the lock until the summer came. Rua overheard his mother saying that by the time his father removed the belt, Pádraig was covered in welts and sores which took months to heal.

"I am going out."

"But you can't, Rua! There's a Red-Moon Curfew."

"I don't care about the prophecy."

"If you are found outside tonight, Rua, you will be shot."

Mona looked at her son. He was a handsome young man: tall and strong too. His hair was a deep red colour and his eyes were bright blue. When Rua was born, his father had named him Jeremiah but when his mother saw his red hair she began to call him Rua and the name stuck.

Ezekiel accepted the nickname willingly. He believed his son was chosen to fulfil the part of the prophecy which said that a boy would be born with flame-red hair who would be the Chosen One. He would have the power to stop the hands of time and protect those who were most in danger on the island of Inis Rua during a blood-red moon.

Ezekiel rejoiced, sure that his redheaded son was the Chosen One.

Mona knew that her wilful son had different ideas from his father, and she feared that those ideas would get him into trouble one day.

Rua Power knew that the Island Keepers were on patrol, but he didn't care. He made his way past the brightly coloured wooden houses, down the dirt track and on towards the one place where he knew no-one would find him.

It was quiet and Rua could hear an owl hooting somewhere in the distance. A fox appeared from out of the bushes and stared straight into his eyes for a moment, before moving on. It was as if it too realised that it was not safe to be out on a night with a blood-red moon.

Rua pulled his green hood up and kept his head down as he walked past the houses in the village. Each one had a single candle flickering in the window to warn off ghosts. He placed his hands in his pockets to keep warm, and as he did so his fingers touched a holy medal that his mother had given him to keep him safe from harm. He traced the outline of the saint's face with his finger as he walked out of the village.

As he got closer to the mountain, it started to snow. He knew that his mother would be worried. He thought of her pacing the floor waiting for him to return. He also knew that she was right to worry. If he were found outside on the night of a blood-red moon, he would be shot despite who his father was.

The Island Keepers were a rugged group of men led by Ezekiel Power. They were armed with guns and they weren't afraid to use them. However, to kill evil spirits they used a Sacred Bow and poisoned arrows which were in Ezekiel's care. No-one ever dared to question their authority for fear of punishment.

As Rua walked towards the mountain, it began to snow harder. He spotted a group of men up ahead. They were holding torches and walking in the direction of Thomas and Agatha Brennans' cottage.

Rua went in the opposite direction, down a small overgrown path that led to the Crooked Forest. And towards the place that people on the island feared the most: the abandoned home of the Witcherly sisters. The villagers would not go near the house as it meant walking through the Crooked Forest. And they feared the ghosts of the sisters, which they believed lingered inside the mould-lined walls of the house.

It was a rundown two-storey house and all the windows were broken as it had not been occupied for a long time. A crooked chimney sat on the roof like a hat. The roof provided an ideal home for the bats and flocks of crows that nested there.

The gate leading to the property was shaped like a heart and was identical to the gate that led into the graveyard on top of the mountain. The house had once belonged to the Witcherly sisters who had lived on the island one hundred years earlier. They died in a fire on top of the mountain and the remains of their bodies were buried in the graveyard with the heart-shaped gates. The two sisters had worked as midwives and tended to the births of the islanders. People feared them as they created remedies from plants growing on the mountainside that were said to have cast spells on people.

Legend said that the two sisters had taken in a group of children to live with them. The children had mysteriously appeared on the island during a blood-red moon. The children had supernatural abilities for which the Witcherly sisters had punished them severely.

Rua often went to the house to be alone and write poetry. He knew that if his parents ever found out that he was practising the creative arts he would be punished. So he hid his books in the loft of the Witcherly sisters' house where he knew that no-one would find them.

The house itself was a hazard. Shards of glass hung from the windows, and the timber beams that held the house together had been eaten away by woodworms.

The hallway was dark and Rua had come prepared. He took a candle and a box of matches from his coat pocket then he struck a match against the wall. The match hissed as it ignited the narrow wick. He held the candle up and walked along the cold, ancient hallway. A speckled mirror hung on the wall, opposite a photograph of two women with thin faces and long black hair that touched the floor. Rua had often studied the photograph and today was no different – he held the candle in front of the photograph and the flickering light from the small flame made it look as though the women's lips were moving. Although the photograph had faded with time, Rua could see the outline of the house in the background. And if he looked closely enough he could just about make out the shape of children's faces peering out of the windows. It looked as though they were pleading with him to help them.

Rua stepped over the broken floorboards and made his way into the sitting room. The empty room smelt bad, worse than usual. Tiny animal carcasses were decaying on the wooden floor. He picked up a piece of bird skull – it was smooth to touch, so he put it into his pocket beside the medal and continued to walk through the house.

Then he glimpsed a glimmer of light. His heart pounded wildly, and he thought that his mother had been right. He should not have gone out on the night of a blood-red moon. Perhaps there was a reason for the Island Keepers patrol after all.

Yet his inquisitive nature drew him on. He walked into the kitchen area.

On the old wooden kitchen table, a candle had been lit and hot wax dripped from it onto a silver candlestick. The wick was burning low but it cast a shadow on a book that sat open on the table. Rua picked up the book. He recognised the brown leather cover. It was his poetry book. A shiver danced up his spine as he realised that someone had left it there. He wondered if his father had found out about his secret hiding place.

He heard a hissing noise coming from behind his back and swung around. He could hear footsteps. They sounded as though they were coming from the roof. Rua looked up at the ceiling but there was nothing there. Then he heard a giggle. He ran towards the front door but found that it was locked. He left the candle down on the floor and tried to pull the door open but no matter how hard he tugged on the handle he could not get out.

"*Help!*" he shouted. Although he knew that no-one could hear him except whoever had locked him in. The Island Keepers were too far away.

He wished he had taken his father's gun with him for protection. Why hadn't he thought of it sooner? Although he knew how to use a gun, he had never shot at anyone or anything before. His target practice was limited to shooting glass bottles off the garden fence. His father told him that he should be out hunting wild animals in preparation for when he became an Island Keeper but Rua could not bring himself to kill anything.

Then Rua screamed as someone grabbed his arms and dragged him backwards, pulling him along the floor and into the sitting room. A nail snagged his trousers as he tried to break free. He kicked his legs and struggled and twisted but it was no use. Rua was a champion boxer and he was able to put up a fight, but he was no match for whoever or whatever had hold of him.

Rua was then thrown violently into a corner of the room. He banged his head against something hard and it stung. He reached up to touch his head and found that it was wet with blood. He thought of his mother back home, lying to his father by pretending that he was asleep in his bed. Rua knew that, as much as his father loved him, he would rather kill him than risk the lives of the people living on Inis Rua. Rua understood the rules now and he wished that he had obeyed them. As Preacher on the island, Rua's father held a great amount of responsibility for the moral conduct of the islanders and he told Rua that he felt personally responsible for their souls. He had a library stacked high with books on ghosts and prophecies and

Rua now was beginning to believe that his father was right and that evil creatures did exist.

He heard someone strike a match and then, one by one, ten large church candles illuminated the room. He blinked as his eyes adjusted to the light. A small mouse scurried across the floorboards and disappeared into a hole in the skirting-board.

Rua shut his eyes and when he opened them again there were three figures in front of him.

The leader of the group was a boy of about Rua's age. He wore a black waistcoat that covered a white shirt. Over that he wore a long coat that reached the floor and heavy black boots. His head was shaved and he had a small birthmark shaped like an apple on his left cheek. In his hand he held a knife. The handle looked as though it had been made from bone and Rua thought that the boy did not look like he was afraid to use it.

Behind the boy was a slightly younger girl. Her hair was so blonde that it appeared silver under the candlelight. A crown of green flowers sat neatly on her head. Her skin looked translucent – Rua could see the blue veins beneath it. Her lips were blood-red. She wore a blue dress that flowed as she moved. Despite her beauty, she had an expression on her face that told him not to trust her.

The youngest girl was about eleven or twelve and had lank brown hair. A black bow had slid down her hair on one side. She wore a silver locket around her neck and a long black dress covered with a white pinafore. There were dark rings under her eyes and her teeth looked sharp when she smiled.

The boy walked over towards Rua and knelt down in front of him, then he placed his knife under Rua's chin and the younger girl laughed.

"Silence, Millie," commanded the boy. He did not take his eyes off Rua for a second. "Who are you?" he demanded.

His voice was deep but Rua did not recognise his accent. He did not speak like an islander or anyone from the mainland that he had heard.

"Answer me!" the boy ordered, prodding the knife into Rua's skin.

The older girl walked up to the boy and placed her hand on his shoulder. She bent and whispered something in his ear. He threw the knife on the ground and walked away, muttering something under his breath.

The girl sat down beside Rua and crossed her legs. She placed her hand on his head and somehow it felt better under her gentle touch.

"I am Ginny," she said.

She had the same accent as the boy and Rua realised that it was an English accent. The only other English people he knew where Thomas and Agatha, the strange couple who lived in Gravedigger's Cottage at the bottom of the mountain. He remembered seeing the Island Keepers visiting them earlier in the evening. Perhaps they knew something about the girl and her strange companions?

"This is Millie."

The little girl smiled at Rua. Then she did the most extraordinary thing. She ran over to the corner of the room and walked up the wall and onto the ceiling.

Rua jumped to his feet and picked the knife up off the floor.

"Millie, down!" Ginny shouted and the little girl jumped off the ceiling and landed on her two feet on the floor. Millie loved showing off her new ghostly trick.

The boy took the knife from Rua, who stood with his mouth wide open, staring at Millie in disbelief. "You won't be needing this."

He then bowed down in front of Rua.

"I am Theo," he said. "And together we are the Magnificent Children."

Theo could not remember where the name 'Magnificent Children' came from, although he had a vague recollection of a circus tent, and the sound of a drum roll, *rat-a-tat-tat, rat-a-tat-tat!* Then there was a man with a black pointy moustache. He stood in the centre of the ring. The audience watched as the tall thin man spoke.

"Ladies and gentlemen, allow me to introduce you to the most Magnificent Children on Earth!"

Theo recalled walking into the ring with Ginny,

Millie and Archie by his side. But that was all he could remember. It was as though his mind was covered in a dense fog.

Rua was speechless.

"Right," said Theo. "Now that you know who we are, who are you?"

"I'm Rua."

Ginny smiled. "We didn't mean to scare you, Rua. We're just wondering what you're doing here in this house, that's all."

"I could ask you the same question. No one has lived in this house for one hundred years! Not since . . ."

"Since what?" asked Theo as he moved the point of the knife under his fingernails to remove the dirt that was lodged there.

"Since the death of the Witcherly sisters."

Millie screamed and began to shake. Ginny ran to her and held her in her arms.

"Don't say their name," Ginny said.

"I'm sorry . . . I didn't . . ."

"It's all right, Millie," soothed Ginny as the girl sobbed into her hair.

"You see, what I'm trying to establish, Rua, is whether you are friend or foe?" Theo kicked a mouse skull across the floor and it smashed against the wall.

"If I can help you, I will," Rua said.

He could not understand what was happening. His father had told him that mysterious creatures came to life on the island during a blood-red moon, but he hadn't believed him.

"Last night Millie and Ginny were shot at – did you have anything to do with that?"

"No, but you are in danger on this island."

Millie began to cry again.

"But why would anyone want to harm us?" asked Ginny.

The moon was low in the sky and shining in through the open window. It illuminated her face. Rua could see that she was crying – he could also see a sprinkling of freckles on her nose that he hadn't noticed earlier.

Theo walked into the kitchen. They all followed him and sat down at the kitchen table.

"Is this yours, Rua?" Ginny asked, pointing to the poetry book.

Rua felt his skin flush, realising there was a strong possibility that she had read his poems.

"Yes." He waited for her to say more but she just stared at Theo.

"Why do they want to hurt us?" Theo said.

"People here believe that when there is a blood-red moon ghosts roam around the island. And because of that my father and the Island Keepers go on patrol. They shoot anyone or anything that moves with a poisoned arrow from a Sacred Bow that has the ability to kill ghosts."

"Your father?" Ginny stood up and pushed the chair across the floor.

"Yes."

"But if he is your father, then how can we trust you? You will lead him to us."

"You have my word. I came here to get away from him. I can't stand all the rules on this island and the sooner I can leave it the better."

Ginny paced up and down the kitchen floor, her shadow falling across Theo as she moved, and Rua was fascinated by the Magnificent Children and their unusual appearance.

"Are we safe here?" Millie asked, rubbing her eyes.

"Yes, this is the safest place on the island," Rua assured her. "No-one ever comes here."

"No-one but you," Theo said, sniggering. Then he swung back on his chair so that it was balancing on two legs.

"But what about Archie?" Millie sobbed.

"Who is Archie?"

"Archie is Millie's brother," Ginny said.

"Where is he now?"

"He is in the cottage at the bottom of the mountain with the man and woman. He was the last to wake and we were forced to leave him behind in the graveyard when we were shot at by the Island Keepers. It was safer to leave him there in his grave than to wait for him."

187

"Oh no!"

"What is it, Rua?" Theo asked.

"I saw my father and a group of Island Keepers making their way over to the cottage. They must know that Archie is there."

Ginny walked over and took Millie's hands.

"Millie, I need you to contact Archie and ask him if he is safe."

"But she can't go over there!" Rua said. "She'll be killed. Have you not listened to a single word I've said?"

"I can speak to Archie without words," said Millie.

"I don't understand."

Theo sighed. "Millie and Archie are twins and they can speak to each other with their minds."

"Thought-reading, you mean?"

"Please be quiet, Rua. Millie needs to concentrate." Ginny stroked Millie's head. "Millie, contact Archie and find out what is happening."

Millie shut her eyes tight. Her eyelids began to flicker as though she was having a dream. The candles went out and the only light in the room was from the moon. The smoke from the candle tickled Rua's throat and he had to hold his breath so that he didn't cough.

"I see him. He is in a dark place with no light, but he is safe." Millie opened her bloodshot eyes and rubbed them with the back of her hand.

"He is safe now. But if my father or the Island Keepers find him, there is nothing we can do to save him." Rua stood up and put his hands in his pockets. "But you are all safe here. The islanders never come to this house."

"You came here," Theo said.

"I am different."

"Why should we trust you?"

"Because you have no other choice. I'll go home, and find out everything I can, and then I'll come back in the morning with food and drink."

The three children looked at each other.

"I don't know," Theo said as he walked out of the kitchen and along the hallway. He rubbed the dust off the photograph on the wall with his fist and stared at the Witcherly sisters.

The girls followed him and Ginny placed her hand on his shoulder.

Rua had come out of the kitchen and he watched Ginny whisper into Theo's ear.

Theo turned to face Rua. "All right, but if you let us down . . ."

"I won't, I promise." Rua held out his hand to Theo.

"I am doing this for you, Ginny, remember that," Theo said.

He spat on his palm and shook Rua's hand.

"A gentlemen's agreement!" Millie clapped and ran up the side of the wall and onto the ceiling.

Rua walked out of the house. An owl hooted. It was perched on the heart-shaped iron gates and its yellow eyes followed his every move. The snow had begun to settle and, as Rua walked back through the forest, he saw footprints that a bird had made in the snow. The Weather Watcher had not forecast snow that night.

Rua could not believe what he had just witnessed. He wondered who the children were, and where they came from. He knew that he had to protect Ginny, Theo and Millie from his father and the Island Keepers. He also knew that he would have to risk his life in the process.

Chapter sixteen

The Island Keepers' Visit

"Thomas, wake up!"

"What is it?"

"Look!"

Agatha was standing at the small square window. Thomas jumped out of bed with fright. He knew that Agatha would not wake him at night unless there was something wrong. The shape of his head remained on the pillow, and the blankets fell onto the floor.

Anger rose in his gut as he looked out of the window.

"Did you wake me up to look at the snow?" Thomas turned to go back to bed.

Agatha tugged at his arm. "It's not the snow. Look, they're coming for us!"

Thomas took a second glance, rubbed the window

and squinted his eyes. This time he saw a burly group of Island Keepers making their way towards Gravedigger's Cottage. They were brandishing torches, and the orange flames flickered like stars against the black sky.

Thomas knew that these men were trouble. He scratched his head and turned to Agatha.

"Did you forget to light the candle?"

"No."

"You didn't leave the house during Lunar Curfew, did you?"

"I haven't been out all night, Thomas, you know that."

"Why are they coming then?" Thomas shouted angrily.

He was beginning to lose patience with Agatha. He could see by the look on her face that she was keeping something from him. He held her by the shoulders.

"This is no time for games, Agatha! Tell me what's going on."

They could hear the sound of footsteps outside the cottage. Thomas glanced at the cuckoo-clock on the mantelpiece. The red-and-green bird walked out, and the clock chimed ten times, which told them that it was ten o'clock. Thomas knew that the Island Keepers were not calling for a friendly talk at this time. They meant business.

"It's Archie. We have to hide him."

"What do you mean?"

"They will take him."

"But –"

"I haven't told you everything, Thomas. Archie died a hundred years ago."

"Have you lost your mind, Agatha? The boy is asleep in bed."

"I can't explain it to you now. But please believe me!"

They heard the sound of loud knocking on the door.

Thomas looked into Aggie's eyes and he quickly realised that the time for questions was later. Now he had to act fast to save the boy.

"Answer the door, Aggie. Try and stall them. I will hide the boy."

Three more loud raps came on the front door. Agatha threw on her green dressing gown and went to open it. Reverend Ezekiel Power stood there with a group of men in the snow.

Reverend Power was a tall, muscular man with a long black beard with thick bristles that reminded Agatha of a sweeping brush – it reached his belt. He had a large nose and small green eyes that were close together. He commanded attention wherever he went, and when he gave a sermon in church on Sunday, his deep, powerful voice put the fear of God into the hearts of all those present.

"Good evening, Mrs Brennan. I am glad to see that you are observing the Lunar Curfew." Ezekiel nodded at the red candlestick in the window of the cottage.

Wax dripped onto the windowsill – the candle was no more than a stub and was about to go out.

"I always do," Agatha said, bowing her head. She pulled her dressing gown closer around her, feeling self-conscious under the Island Keeper's watchful gaze.

"How is your fine husband tonight?"

"Thomas?"

"Unless you have any other husbands we don't know about."

The men laughed. Ezekiel placed his hands over his stomach and Agatha smiled despite her pounding heart.

"May we come in and speak with him, please?"

Agatha knew that something wasn't right – they were too polite. She could tell that they were trying to catch her out. She would have to remain vigilant and not say anything that would lead them to Archie. It wasn't just his life at risk now. She and Thomas could be killed too.

"Yes, of course." She pulled back the door and her heart sank as the men stepped inside.

Thomas appeared in the doorway of Archie's bedroom. He shut the bedroom door behind him.

"Good evening, gentlemen. What can we do for you?" Thomas smiled and rubbed his hands together, as though he were greeting old friends.

His voice was strained. Agatha prayed that the Island Keepers did not pick up on it. She walked over and stood by her husband's side.

"Have you noticed anything strange up in the graveyard lately?" Ezekiel looked straight into Thomas's eyes.

"No, I can't say I have. Can I get you a drink, gentlemen? Aggie, make some tea."

"We are not here for tea, thank you, Mr and Mrs Brennan." Reverend Power walked around the kitchen. "We are conducting routine searches of the area. There has been some suspicious activity lately in the graveyard. And with the blood-red moon in the sky, we have to remain vigilant."

Thomas and Agatha sat down at the kitchen table. Thomas held Agatha's hand and smiled reassuringly at her while Ezekiel Power and the Island Keepers ransacked their kitchen. They looked inside every cupboard and emptied every drawer onto the floor. They broke cups and plates. Agatha started to cry – it was all too much for her.

"What is this?"

Thomas looked at Agatha, and they both turned to Ezekiel Power, who was holding Archie's red coat which had been hanging on the back of a chair.

"I didn't know you had children."

"I'm sorry?" said Agatha.

"Children, Mrs Brennan. I said I didn't know that you had any." Ezekiel stood on a broken plate, and it crunched beneath his boot.

"Yes," said Aggie.

"No," said Thomas.

"Which is it now? Surely you must know whether you have children or not?"

The men watched intently as Agatha spoke.

"What we meant to say was, yes, we did have a child, a son. Walter. But he was killed."

"Ah yes, I do recall Mrs Power telling me about your boy. The war, wasn't it? Sorry for your loss, Mrs Brennan. I have two boys of my own. I don't know what I would do without them. A moment's silence, gentlemen, please."

The Island Keepers bowed their heads. Then Reverend Power uttered a prayer.

"Dear Lord, bless these good people and protect them from the wicked ghosts that roam our island. Amen."

"Amen," the Island Keepers repeated.

"You won't mind if we check the rest of the cottage?" Ezekiel's voice was gentler this time. He felt sorry for Thomas and Agatha; he could see that the death of their only son had taken its toll on them.

"Go ahead," said Thomas.

Ezekiel gestured to the Island Keepers to stay where they were. Then he opened the door to Thomas and Agatha's bedroom. He stepped inside and did a swift search, then came out and walked into Archie's room.

Agatha held her breath and rested her head on

Thomas's shoulder. She waited to hear Archie scream and was shocked when Ezekiel Power walked out alone.

"Nothing unusual here. I'm sorry to have troubled you."

He walked out the door of the cottage and the Island Keepers followed him.

"You were asking about the graveyard?" Thomas said as he held the door open.

"Three of the graves have been disturbed. The bodies are gone."

"Gone?" said Agatha.

"Taken from their graves."

Ezekiel picked up the shovel that was at the entrance to the cottage and ran his finger over the metal edge to check if it had any traces of mud on it, which would indicate that it had been used recently.

"A terrible thing," Agatha said.

"Yes. If you good people notice anything strange, please contact me. After all, whoever did this would have walked right past your cottage."

"Of course we will," said Aggie.

"Goodnight, Mr and Mrs Brennan."

"Goodnight, gentlemen," said Thomas.

As Thomas was shutting the door Reverend Power turned back and Agatha's heart sank.

"See you on Sunday then," he said.

It was compulsory for all islanders to attend church on Sundays.

"Of course, Reverend Power," said Agatha.

Thomas shut the wooden door and bolted it. They watched silently as the Island Keepers left, then they both ran into Archie's bedroom.

There was no sign of Archie.

"Where is he?" cried Agatha.

Thomas pointed at the fireplace and Agatha was amazed to see a pair of black boots dangling down the chimney.

Thomas helped Archie out of his hiding place and he ran into Agatha's open arms. He was sweating, and he was black with soot from the chimney.

"Thank goodness they didn't find you!" Agatha sobbed.

She rocked him back and forth in her arms. She did not care that he was covered in soot – all that mattered to her was that he was safe. She decided not to bath him until the next day in case the Island Keepers decided to return. Instead she sang to him until he fell asleep.

Chapter seventeen

Empty Graves

Agatha woke up in a cold sweat. The blood-red moon shone in through her bedroom window and cast a warm glow on her husband's face. She watched the even rise and fall of his chest which told her that he was in a deep sleep. He did not wake as Agatha slipped from the bed. She picked up a green woollen blanket off the chair in the corner of the room and walked into the kitchen. Her wedding photograph hung on the wall. She hardly recognised herself in it. She lit a candle, the night air sending a shiver down her spine. Then she made her way to the boy's bedroom.

The fire had long since gone out, but amber coals still glowed in the grate. Archie was asleep. Agatha wondered how it was possible for a ghost to sleep. Perhaps she was losing her mind, she thought. Grief can do such things. After all, there was no such thing as a ghost. She looked at Archie, his left arm thrown above his head. His face was turned away from her, but she could still see the blue vein visible beneath his translucent skin. The blankets were tangled around his ankles, and his right hand poked out over the edge of the bed. He looked very much like a real boy, yet there was something otherworldly about him.

Agatha knew one way that she could prove for certain that Archie was a ghost. Then perhaps Thomas would believe her. She could see the fear in Thomas's eyes and knew he thought that she had gone mad. Like the time he'd caught her trying to communicate with Walter after he had died. But this was different and, who knew, if Archie came back from the dead, didn't that mean there was a possibility Walter could too?

She touched Archie's forehead. His skin felt clammy, so she covered him with the green blanket. She left him sleeping and crept out of the room, being careful to avoid the creaking floorboards.

In the kitchen she sat at the table and put on her boots. There was a hole in the sole of the left one and she knew the snow would get in. But there was nothing she could do about that now; she would have to repair it later. The clock ticked on the mantelpiece. Agatha could feel the blood rush to her head and her heart thumped in her chest. She put her coat on and bit her bottom lip. Then, while Thomas and Archie slept, she crept outside. She stood in a pool of light from the blood-red moon and watched as it reflected off the snow.

The mountain loomed overhead. Agatha could make out the black silhouette of the cross that marked the graveyard.

She imagined what the Island Keepers would do to her if they found her out of her cottage on the night of a Lunar Curfew. They would accuse her of witchcraft and drown her in the ocean. She shuddered at the thought. She knew she had to go to church and be seen to lead a good Christian life.

The snow got deeper the farther she walked. Water leaked through her boot. Her toes squelched inside her stockings. Dotted on the mountainside were cottages that had been abandoned during the Famine. Their roofs were missing. It looked as though a giant had walked past and pulled them off. The stone walls that surrounded them were crumbling. Agatha had often imagined how families of seven or eight people had lived in such small homes. She also thought of the men who had built the stone walls, all those years ago. Hard-working men, like Thomas.

Halfway up the mountain, a stone got into Agatha's boot and her foot began to bleed. She considered turning back, but she knew the only way she could help Archie was to find out where he came from. Two donkeys stood on the mountainside; they raised their heads as if to acknowledge Agatha. Their hoofs were covered in snow. Their tails swished back and forth, like sweeping brushes across a dusty floor.

By the time Agatha reached the mountaintop, she was out of breath and a pain darted across her side. She looked down at her wet clothes. The cold had seeped into her boots and her toes were numb.

It had taken her longer than she had expected to reach the graveyard. Daylight was beginning to break. The birds were chirping and the black clouds had parted to reveal a pale blue sky. She watched a blackbird as it made footprints in the snow. She looked back at where she had come from. She could see her home at the bottom of the mountain. Beyond that she could make out the village and the shape of other cottages, those owned by the Island Keepers. They stretched out to the sea, which looked like black ink on the horizon. She heard a cat cry in the distance – it sounded like a newborn baby's cry, and it unsettled her.

When Agatha had regained her strength, she turned to face the graveyard. A stone wall surrounded it. The heart-shaped iron gate came into view. It looked like something out of a fairytale. Agatha tugged at the bolt. At first she thought she would be unable to open it. Then she tugged harder, and it came loose. The gate squeaked as she opened it and walked into the graveyard.

Agatha saw something move behind the headstone closest to her. She hid behind an oak tree and watched a beautiful fox walk across her path, and out of the gate.

Agatha walked through the graveyard, her eyes scanning the headstones.

Then she found the empty graves.

A mound of dirt sat beside each headstone, covered in snow. Agatha looked down into the first empty grave in astonishment.

A brown owl with yellow eyes stared at her from the oak tree, but she did not see it. She hunkered down beside the headstone, being careful not to fall into the open grave. She rubbed the snow off the headstone with the sleeve of her coat, and read its inscription:

Here lies
Archibald Luxbridge
Born 1836
Died 1848
Age 12 years

And his sister Mildred Luxbridge
Born 1836
Died 1848
Age 12 years

She gasped as the realisation hit her that the little boy lying in bed in her cottage was Archie Luxbridge. She cried as she thought of him and his sister Millie lying in the cold grave for one hundred years. Then she thought of her son Walter lying in his grave and cried for him too.

Agatha shivered as the wet snow soaked through her clothes. She stood up and walked over to the second grave.

This time the gravestone read:

Here lies
Theodore Grime
Born 1834
Died 1848
Age 14 years

The third grave belonged to a girl:

Here lies
Genevieve Potter
Born 1835
Died 1848
Age 13 years

Then Agatha heard the gate creak and realised that someone else was in the graveyard. She stood still, afraid to move. She knew that if the Island Keepers had followed her, they would think she had something to do with the empty graves. And worse still, they would punish Thomas too. She felt angry with herself for not covering her tracks more carefully.

"Agatha, are you here?"

Agatha sighed in relief when she heard her husband's voice.

"What on earth are you doing?"

"Thomas, look!"

Thomas looked at the recently disturbed graves. He hadn't noticed them on the night that he found Archie as he hadn't gone that far into the graveyard.

"Who would do such a thing?"

"That's not all."

Thomas followed his wife over to the first grave. The grave of Archibald and Mildred Luxbridge.

"Look, it's Archie's grave."

Thomas rubbed his chin with his hand. He stood still for what seemed like a long time and then he shook his head.

"I told you, Thomas."

He walked over to Agatha, grabbed her by the shoulders and shook her hard, harder than he meant to. He felt so angry. He thought he had put all this behind him when they moved to the island. And now it was all happening again.

"Do you realise what you're saying, Agatha? You're saying that the boy asleep in our cottage is dead, and that he's a ghost."

"I know it sounds –"

"It sounds ridiculous, Aggie, that's what it sounds!"

Thomas walked away from his wife and paced up and down the graveyard. He rubbed the back of his head with his hand.

Agatha was furious with Thomas. He had seen Archie's empty grave with his own two eyes and yet he still did not believe her.

To take her mind off her husband, she read the inscription on the next grave she came to and it read:

> Here lies
> Petulia Witcherly
> Born 1800
> Died 1848
> Age 48 years
>
> And her sister
> Maud Witcherly
> Born 1808
> Died 1848
> Age 40 years

The grave belonged to the Witcherly sisters. Agatha knew that they had lived in the haunted house in the crooked forest. She had heard of them from the villagers and also from Archie who had told her the Witcherly sisters were responsible for his death and the deaths of his sister Millie and two other children,

Ginny and Theo. Agatha could not understand why these wicked women were buried in the same graveyard as the children.

A thought suddenly occurred to her: along with Archie there were three more children missing from their graves. Agatha vowed to do everything in her power to find them.

Thomas watched his wife as she read the inscription. She looked frail and old, much older than she was. Thomas was a God-fearing man and, up until this point, he had thought that perhaps Agatha had lost her mind. However, as he stood in the graveyard that morning and stared into Archie's grave, he could not find a logical explanation for its emptiness. And he came to the realisation that Agatha's theory was as good as any.

Chapter eighteen

The Crooked Forest

Archie stood in front of the Witcherly sisters' rundown home. He had his back to the Crooked Forest. The forest got its unusual name due to the shape of the oak trees, which were bent like hooks. Their roots clawed beneath the soil, like broken fingernails trying to hold on to a ledge of a cliff. The sun never shone in the Crooked Forest; the trees held up their leaves to block out the light. Their curved trunks were bent like the backs of old men. Legends told of people venturing into the forest and never coming out again. The islanders rarely entered it and children growing up on the island were fearful of the crooked trees, which emerged like a scar on the otherwise perfect landscape.

The east wind blew the leaves off the sun-starved

trees. They spread their bare branches like bony fingers into the low, orange sky.

Archie looked up at the crooked chimney that prodded the horse-shaped clouds. A bat hung upside down from the roof. Its wings were folded across its chest like an envelope. Two pointy ears stuck out from its triangular-shaped face.

A flock of crows with oily feathers and sharp beaks circled overhead. The biggest crow had a dent in its beak and was missing its left foot. Archie watched as it swooped down like an arrow in flight and dissected the carcass of a small, brown fieldmouse that lay in the snow. Pink entrails hung from smooth, white bones like washing on a line.

There was something familiar about the dilapidated house. Archie felt as though he had been there before somehow, although he could not remember when.

An iron gate covered in ivy stood at the entrance to the property and it was shaped like a heart, just like the gate that led into the graveyard on top of the mountain.

Archie opened the gate and stepped inside. A stone footpath led straight to the Witcherlys' front door. Each flagstone was shaped like a heart. Green weeds and nettles appeared through the cracks in the path like unwanted guests at a party.

An owl hooted in an oak tree – his yellow eyes followed Archie along the path and up to the house.

The front door was red. A silver door knocker in the shape of a lion's head with a silver ring between its teeth sat waiting to be used.

Archie took the silver ring in his hand and stared at the lion with the silver mane which appeared to be blowing in the breeze. Then he pulled his hand free and banged on the door three times with his fist instead.

The crows screeched and formed a circle above his head. Archie shivered and tugged at his red coat. He thought it strange that there was no response. He knew that Millie, Theo and Ginny were expecting him so he pushed the door and, finding it open, he walked inside.

The front door snapped shut behind him. The hallway was dark and uninviting and it took a moment for his eyes to adjust to the lack of light.

He traced his fingers along the damp wall and walked along the dark hallway. The house smelt of rotten eggs and urine. Archie pinched his nose with his fingers and tried to breathe through his mouth.

An oval-shaped mirror hung from a chain on the wall. The glass was speckled with black spots. Archie looked into the mirror but he did not see his reflection. All he could see was the crumbling brick wall behind him which was green with mould.

He ran his fingers through his hair. Then he placed his finger over a small crack in the corner of the glass.

A single tear fell from his eye as he realised that without a shadow of a doubt he was dead.

The sound of laughter echoed down the winding staircase that stood in the centre of the hallway. Archie recognised Millie's voice straight away and he wiped away the tear with the back of his hand.

As he climbed the stairs, he cut his finger on a nail that stuck out from the bannister. Bright-red blood fell like rain onto the staircase. Archie sucked the blood from his finger. It stung and the blood tasted bitter in his mouth. He wondered how he could bleed if he was a ghost.

Halfway up the stairs there was a small landing. Archie paused at a writing desk with two small drawers in the front of it. On top of the desk was a leather-bound book. Archie picked it up. It was covered with a layer of dust. He blew the dust away and coughed, then opened the book and flicked through the yellow pages. A red ribbon led him to a page in the centre of the book.

At first Archie thought it was a cookery book as there were lists of ingredients, but as he read on he realised it was a book of spells and potions. The first spell in the book was a potion to prevent supernatural ability in godless children.

Archie's stomach lurched and his finger throbbed. It had started to bleed again. A dark red stain appeared like ink on the yellow page. He placed the

211

book back on the writing desk, then noticed a peculiar-looking object on the desk.

It was a small glass dome filled with water, resting on a black base. Archie noticed miniature figures inside the dome. As he moved it to get a closer look, small particles floated in the water. They looked like tiny snowflakes drifting from the sky. He shook the dome and realised that the snowflakes were made from tiny fragments of bone. Six miniature figures made of porcelain stood in front of a house.

As Archie looked, he noticed the heart-shaped gate, the crooked chimney and the oak tree. He realised that it was the Witcherly sisters' house. Archie gulped as he looked at the tiny figures. Each one was perfectly formed.

The first one was a boy in a red riding coat and black boots. He held the hand of a girl with lank hair which was secured into place with a bow. The girl looked as though she was crying. In front of the oak tree sat a girl with long, blonde hair. She wore a crown of green flowers and a blue dress, and a gold rope hung from her waist. Another boy had a scar on his face, and dark eyes. They were miniature figures of Millie, Ginny, Theo and himself. Archie could not understand how that was possible. In the doorway were two identical women. Their long, black hair stretched down as far as their bare feet. They wore black dresses and had red capes draped around their shoulders. The capes were secured with silver brooches shaped like swords.

Archie looked away from the miniature house and then looked back: it still looked the same. A wave of nausea spread through his body and he thought he might get sick.

Then he heard a loud scratching noise above his head. He turned to look up at the ceiling and saw Millie hanging upside down with her arms folded across her chest.

"Do you see the bat, Archie?" Millie giggled. Strands of her hair stretched down like stalactites.

"Get down this instant!"

Millie did as she was told and landed on her feet beside her brother, but she crossed her arms and stamped her foot in protest.

A scream coming from upstairs alerted the children to the fact that something was wrong.

Archie held on tight to the snow globe. The fragments of bone swirled around in a snowstorm as he ran up the stairs, Millie at his heels.

The scream had come from a room at the top of the stairs.

Archie and Millie rushed inside.

The roof sloped down on either side of the small room and Archie could see at a glance that it had been a nursery.

Ginny was crouched in the corner of the room

where the roof was lowest. Archie and Millie could see she was studying the wooden beam which led up to the ceiling. Theo stood in the centre of the room, the apple-shaped birthmark on his cheek red under the light.

Archie hid the snow globe behind his back with his left hand as he and Millie went over to Ginny.

"What's wrong?" he asked.

Ginny turned to face him. Her face was pale, and her lips were deep red.

"It's this." She pointed to the wooden beam.

At first Archie thought she was referring to the tiny holes in the wood, made by woodworm.

"The woodworm?"

"Not that. Look!"

Carved into the wooden beam were the children's names: *Ginny, Theo, Millie, Archie.* Underneath the names the word *HELP* was written in capital letters.

"Why are our names on this piece of wood?" Millie asked.

Theo bit the corner of his fingernail. He could not explain what was happening and he was starting to feel scared, although he didn't want the others to know that.

"Does anyone know how we got here?" Ginny's teeth chattered and her body shuddered.

"Calm down, Ginny," said Theo. "We'll work it out together, but you have to calm down."

Archie was examining the room. A dapple-grey horse rested on a bow-shaped rocker beneath the window. There was a brown saddle on its back; it was the perfect size for a child. Beside that was a large wooden doll's house. It was three storeys high and painted green. Archie crouched down to peer into one of the upstairs windows and saw a tiny doll sitting on a miniature dapple-grey rocking horse. There was a tiny table set for tea, a bookshelf in the corner and a grandfather clock.

Archie stood up too quickly and hit his head on the ceiling.

There were four beds, one in each corner of the room. A pewter candlestick with a brass handle stood on a table. Beside it was a copy of a book by an author called Jonathan Swift. The title of the book was *Travels into Several Remote Nations of the World. In Four Parts. By Lemuel Gulliver, First a Surgeon, and then a Captain of Several Ships*. There was also a penny coin with the young Queen Victoria's side profile on it. Archie picked the coin up and placed it into his pocket, beside a small St Brigid's cross he had taken from Agatha's house. Then he rubbed his finger over Queen Victoria's face.

Theo grabbed Archie's shoulder. "What do you know about all this?"

"Nothing – why?"

"Don't give me that nonsense or I'll …"

Theo pushed Archie and he fell against the doll's house. He grabbed a handful of Archie's hair with his fist. The snow globe fell from Archie's hand and rolled across the floor. It didn't stop until it hit the rocking horse.

"What's this?"

Theo picked the snow globe off the floor. He looked into it and saw the porcelain figurines in the snow, although he did not recognise the house or the figures. Archie's heart thumped in his chest and he sighed with relief when Theo walked away from him and placed the snow globe on the shelf beside the book and candlestick.

Millie was looking at her name carved in the wooden beam above the word 'HELP'.

Archie sat on the floor and placed his head in his hands. Ginny sat down beside him and put her arm around his shoulders, then glared at Theo with hot angry tears in her eyes.

"Please, Archie, tell us what you know," Ginny said. Her voice shook but was gentle as she spoke to the boy.

"I was wandering around in a graveyard and the man in the cottage brought me home with him and I had to hide when the bad men came."

"Bad men?" A look of fear flashed in Ginny's eyes as she realised that they were in danger.

"They said that the bodies were taken from the graves," Archie said.

Ginny rubbed her neck with the back of her hand. The islanders were looking for them. If only she could remember everything that had happened. But there were large gaps in her memory.

"We are dead, Ginny," said Archie.

"Dead?"

"Yes."

Ginny knew deep down that what Archie was saying was true. However, the idea of being a ghost frightened her and she wanted more than anything for them both to be wrong.

"But how can we be dead, Archie?"

"I remember being here before, more than a lifetime ago. I see pictures in my mind of another time."

"You get them too?" Ginny jumped to her feet and Blue flew out into the air. "Mine feel like dreams. There are people dressed in brightly coloured clothes – they look like they belong to a circus. Then I am standing on top of the mountain and there is a big fire."

"I've seen the fire too," said Archie.

Blue flew around the room. A yellow feather drifted through the air. Ginny could tell that the little bird was distressed. She held out her hand and Blue perched on her wrist. The branches of the oak tree tapped against the window and cast a shadow on the floor.

Theo looked out of the window. He could see the mountain in the distance. He too had been having bad dreams.He remembered an old woman with eyes that

217

rolled across the floor and a man called Mr Moonshine who played the violin. There were other things too but they scared him and he was not going to admit that to the others.

"Where's Millie?"

Archie ran towards the door.

"It's all right, Archie – I'll go to her."

Ginny needed time to think about what she had just heard. Could it be true?

She walked from room to room and Blue flew behind her. But Millie was nowhere to be seen.

As Ginny walked down the stairs she had the unnerving feeling that someone was following her. She turned her head quickly, but there was no one there.

She noticed the flecks of blood on the staircase from where Archie had cut his finger, and she quickened her pace and ran into the kitchen. It had started to snow again. The rocking chair was rocking back and forth and the back door was wide open.

Ginny ran outside and saw Millie lying beneath the branches of the oak tree. The wind blew Ginny's skirt up to her knees and she had to hold it down with her hand. Her crown blew away. Millie looked so peaceful, like an angel lying in the white snow.

"You'll catch your death out here," Ginny said, immediately regretting her choice of words.

"I'm already dead."

"Don't say that, Millie."

"It's true."

"How do you know?"

"I can feel it and I know that you can too."

Ginny lay down beside Millie and looked up at the branches of the tree as they swayed in the wind.

"I found something, Ginny."

Millie sat up and placed a black-and-white photograph in Ginny's hands. Ginny looked at the photograph. It looked like it had been taken a long time ago in the bedroom of the Witcherly house. The year 1848 was written on the back in pencil.

In the photograph Ginny was sitting in the bedroom brushing Millie's hair. A woman with long, black hair had her arms stretched out and was standing behind them, her fingernails so long that they curled at the ends. But both the girls seemed unaware of her presence or that they were being photographed.

"Where did you find this, Millie?" Ginny sat up. Her hair was covered in snowflakes.

"It was in a box under the bed."

"Which bed?"

"In the room we were in."

"Did you show this to Theo?"

"No."

"Are you sure, Millie?"

"Yes! Are you angry with me, Ginny?"

"No, Millie, I'm not angry. I'm scared. "

Ginny glanced up at the bedroom window. Theo

was looking down at them. His face was pressed against the glass. It appeared distorted, his eyes like black slits and his teeth bulging from red gums like tombstones. Ginny turned her head away, hoping that Millie had not noticed him.

"Come on, Millie, let's go back inside."

Ginny took Millie's hand and they walked back into the house. Although Ginny did not know what the future held, she had a bad feeling that something terrible was on the horizon. And it would only be a matter of time before it caught up with them.

Chapter nineteen

The Ghost in the Graveyard

Rua walked up the mountainside as he had done many times before. The snow had begun to melt, and tufts of green grass appeared in patches beneath his feet.

The cold wind blew on his cheeks, and his fingers felt numb. He remembered playing hide and seek behind the headstones in the graveyard as a boy, and he had often wondered about the children who were buried there. He imagined who they were and what they looked like. Was it possible that the children in the Witcherly sisters' home had slept in these graves for one hundred years?

Rua opened the heart-shaped gate and stepped inside. His fingers were cold, and he could see his breath in the air. There were tracks in the snow that looked as though they had been made by a small bird – perhaps a robin.

Rua walked reluctantly towards the back of the graveyard. He was afraid that his worst fears were about to be confirmed, yet he felt compelled to go there to see for himself if the graves belonged to the children.

It was easy to tell the children's graves as each had a mound of earth beside it.

Rua walked over to the one that had always fascinated him the most.

There was the image of a single rose carved into the stone headstone. He touched it and ran his finger along each of the letters of the name.

Genevieve Potter
Born 1835
Died 1848
Age 13 years

Rua fell to his knees and looked into the empty grave. It was hard to believe that Ginny had lain there beneath the ground for one hundred years. She died when she was thirteen years old; that was two years younger than he was now. His mother had told him that when someone died young, they stayed that way forever.

He wondered if Ginny had left a mother and father

behind to mourn for her. Even as Rua sat by her graveside he still found it hard to believe that she was dead. She looked so alive to him. With her blonde hair that resembled strands of silver. Then there was her pale skin and piercing blue eyes. There were so many questions that needed answers. Such as how had she died? And how did she arrive on the island in the first place? They were all questions he needed to ask Ginny. None of it made any sense but there was one niggling question that worried him the most: why did he feel such a strong bond to these ghost children?

Something caught Rua's eye. A shard of sunlight shone on an object that lay glistening in the pile of soil. It was a gold cross and chain. Rua knew that it must have belonged to Ginny, as it was next to her grave. He picked it up and rubbed the soil off it. The chain was fragile. He held it between his fingers and stood up.

"So it's true then," came a hushed voice.

Rua turned around and saw Ginny standing there. It occurred to him that she didn't look like a ghost, not really, not like in the ghost stories that his brother used to tell him. She was made of flesh and bones and she looked like a real girl, although her blue dress looked as though it came from another time.

Rua had terrible nightmares as a child. He dreamt that he saw a faceless ghost floating above him in the darkness. Holding out her hands to him and begging him to go with her. He would see his father there in the shadows, pulling him back. Rua would wake up sweating, his heart pounding, and his mother would run to him and hold him in her arms until he drifted off to sleep again. He wondered if he was having a bad dream now. Although as he watched Ginny kneeling at the graveside, he realised that he was not afraid of ghosts any more.

Ginny leant forward and peered inside, and for a second Rua thought she was going to fall in. He fell on his knees beside her and grabbed her arm. She turned to him, shocked that he had touched her, and she pulled her arm away.

"I'm sorry, I thought . . ."

"What? That I was going to fall in?"

"Yes, I suppose I did."

"I can't believe that I lay in that grave for one hundred years." Ginny's eyes glistened with tears. Her pale cheeks were flushed. "That would make me one hundred and thirteen years old."

The wind whistled in the trees. Ginny looked into Rua's eyes and Rua looked towards the sky as he thought he heard the sound of a bird singing. She rested her head against his shoulder and they both watched as the clouds moved slowly across the sky.

"Do you think we can die twice, Rua?"

"I don't know – although they say that cats have nine lives so I suppose it's possible."

"I don't want to die again."

"Do you remember how you died?" The words had tripped eagerly off Rua's tongue before he had time to think about them.

Ginny pulled away from him and stood up. Her dress was covered in mud and torn at the shoulder. She walked over to the stone wall that surrounded the graveyard. Then she sat down beside a statue of an angel. A spider was spinning a silver web on the angel's wings. A black fly was trapped in the silver threads.

Rua followed Ginny and sat down beside her. He hoped that he hadn't scared her away; his mother always told him that he should think before he spoke.

The angel's hands were joined in prayer and pointed towards heaven. A crow screeched overhead, and they both looked towards the sky. Then a fox walked through the graveyard, and Rua wondered if the fox was a ghost too.

"Sometimes I have memories – they are like dreams," she said.

"Memories about how you died?" Rua asked.

"Not really. They're more about how I lived. Or at least that's what I think they are. I am in a tent with a red-and-white dome."

"Like a circus tent."

"Yes. I mean, I think so."

"Are you on your own in the memory, Ginny?"

Ginny was deep in thought. Three frown lines converged on her forehead as she recalled fragments

225

of her life. A life that took place one hundred years earlier.

"No, Theo is there, and Millie and Archie."

Rua didn't trust Theo. He wasn't as friendly as the other children. Rua guessed that he was jealous of him, afraid that Rua wanted to take his place as leader of the little group. But Rua just wanted to help all of them as he was the only hope that these Magnificent Ghosts had of surviving on the island.

"Did you go to see the circus, Ginny?"

"I don't know, Rua." Ginny bit her lip as she concentrated her mind. A spot of blood appeared in the corner of her mouth. "But, I am not here."

"On this island, you mean?"

"I was somewhere else, Rua." Ginny smiled as she started to piece the memories together. One by one like pieces in a jigsaw puzzle.

"Before you came here?"

"Yes, I think it was a city. There were crowds of people and a liger."

"A liger?" Rua had never heard of a liger before and thought that perhaps Ginny was getting confused. But he did not say anything more.

"There are other memories too . . . of the house."

"The Witcherly house?"

"Yes, bad memories, Rua."

Ginny looked away as she recalled the wicked Witcherly sisters.

Then Rua remembered the cross and chain he still had in his right hand.

"Is this yours, Ginny?" He handed it to her.

"Yes, it looks familiar."

"Let me put it on you."

Ginny lifted her long blonde hair and Rua placed the chain around her pale neck and secured the small gold clasp.

"I have an idea, Ginny."

Ginny turned to face him, her eyes wide in anticipation.

"In my father's library, there are books, ancient books. They hold the secrets of the Blood-Red Moon Prophecy and the Lunar Curfew."

"What's the Blood-Red Moon Prophecy, Rua? Does it have something to do with me and the others?"

"Something happened on this island one hundred years ago, Ginny, something bad that ended in the deaths of four children. It has to be in the books."

"Will your father allow you to read them?"

"No. And if he finds out I was in the library he might link me to you. And then I won't be able to help you or the other children, Ginny."

Rua watched her as she considered what he had just said to her.

"What about the people that Archie met – Thomas and Agatha? Can we trust them?" she asked.

"They are outsiders here so I think that we can trust them."

"I hope you're right, Rua."

A cool breeze blew the leaves of the trees, and Ginny stood up and walked over to her headstone. Rua followed her. She placed her fingers into the smooth crevices of the carved stone and traced her name. Then a tear fell from her eye and landed six feet below her in the open grave.

She took Rua's hand and placed it on her ribcage.

"Do you feel anything, Rua?"

"I can feel your heartbeat, Ginny. But doesn't that mean you are alive?"

"It's not the sound of my heart beating, Rua. That stopped one hundred years ago. It is Blue, beating his wings against my ribcage."

Rua pulled his hand away. Ginny looked into Rua's eyes; she felt that she could trust him with her secret, but she didn't want to scare him.

"I was born with a special ability, Rua."

"What kind of ability, Ginny?"

"It is hard to explain. Perhaps it would be better if I showed you."

Ginny stepped back and began to cough. Rua was worried as he thought that she was choking. She knelt down and coughed more. Rua was thinking she was about to get sick when a feather came out of her mouth and drifted down into the open grave.

Then a small blue and yellow bird flew from her mouth. It glided through the air and landed on

Ginny's headstone. Then it opened its beak and began to sing.

Ginny waited for Rua to respond. He was shocked for a few moments, but then a smile erupted on his lips.

"How did you do that? I mean, how can a bird live inside you?"

"My ribcage is shaped like a birdcage, Rua. Blue has always lived inside me."

The sky was beginning to turn dark like a purple bruise. From where they were standing they could see the waves colliding with the shore. Ginny shivered, and Rua gave her his green coat.

"Put this on, Ginny – you're cold."

"Thank you, Rua."

"We had better go back down the mountain. It's getting late. The Island Keepers will be on patrol soon."

Rua looked up: the blood-red moon was emerging like a ruby in the darkening sky.

Ginny opened her mouth, and Blue flew back inside her ribcage.

Ginny and Rua walked down the mountain together. Ginny was unsure of her past and even less certain about her future, but she felt happy that she had the present moment and she had found a strong friend who would keep her and the other children safe.

Chapter twenty

The Unexpected Guest

Agatha paced up and down the kitchen floor while Thomas lit the fire. The sun was setting in the sky and an orange glow entered the cottage window and cast a light on the floor. Agatha lit the gas-lamp. It made a popping sound as the flame ignited. Then she placed a red candle on the window-ledge. Stan was stretched out on the mat, waiting for the heat from the fire to warm him up.

"Sit down, Agatha," Thomas said. Then he stood up with difficulty and placed his hand on the lower part of his back.

She sat on the three-legged stool near the window.

Agatha was restless. She had been unable to sleep since the Island Keepers had searched the cottage. She hated the sight of the red moon and the way that it appeared like a bloodstain in the black sky each night. She felt nervous so she chewed on her fingernails and jumped at the slightest sound.

Whenever the branch from a tree scratched at the window pane, or the wind howled down the chimney, Agatha thought that the Island Keepers had returned. She had dreamt that she was dragged from her bed in the middle of the night and taken deep into the Crooked Forest. Then she was tied to a tree and left to starve to death and large black crows swooped down and pecked her eyes out. She dreaded to think what the Island Keepers would do to the children when they found them.

Each night, while Thomas was sleeping, Agatha crept from her bed. She padded along the floorboards in her bare feet and peered out of the kitchen window. She knew for certain that the Island Keepers would return. It was only a matter of time and she was terrified.

A fox had started to visit her and somehow it made her feel safe. Each night the small red animal appeared from the shadows. It darted in and out of the trees and stared at Agatha. She felt as though it was trying to tell her something. She left out scraps of food for it – red berries and pieces of leftover meat. Recently it started to venture closer to the cottage and occasionally when the door was open the animal came inside. But never when Thomas was home. Its fur smelt of the forest, damp earth and pine needles.

Agatha wondered if the fox was her son Walter. She had heard of reincarnation and thought that perhaps he had come back to life in the shape of a fox. Although deep down she knew that the animal was just cold and hungry. She had started to call the fox Walter, and it didn't seem to object. Agatha did not say this to anyone as she knew that they wouldn't understand. She decided to keep the fox a secret for a while longer and had started to look forward to the animal's nightly visits.

Agatha had considered paying a visit to Ezekiel's wife Mona and pleading with her to help the children – after all, she was a mother herself. But Agatha didn't know if she could trust the woman and decided it would be better to lay low for a while.

Now, sitting in the kitchen with Thomas, she asked, "Thomas, how can we help the children?" She could not get Archie and Millie out of her mind.

Thomas stretched – his lower back ached. He wasn't as young as he used to be. He walked over to his wife and brushed her hair out of her eyes. He had seen her like this before – after Walter had died. The doctor had diagnosed her with melancholia, which he said was brought on by grief. Thomas hoped it wasn't happening again.

"Agatha, they are not children."

"Don't give me that, Thomas Brennan! You carried Archie here on your back, we fed him and bathed him.

He slept under our roof!" Then she walked over to the chair beside the fire and sat down, with her head in her hands.

Thomas knelt in front of her. Stan purred, then he arched his back and walked away. An amber flame danced in the grate and the fire crackled.

"They are dead, Agatha. Just like Walter."

A tap on the front door startled them. Agatha jumped up.

Thomas got a fright too, but he didn't want Agatha to know that he was scared so he rose to his feet calmly and walked to the door.

"Be careful, Thomas! It could be the Island Keepers," Agatha warned.

Thomas opened the door and looked at Rua standing there. He knew he was Ezekiel's son. He was a tall boy of about fifteen years of age. He looked like a miniature version of his father, although he had bright-red hair and grey eyes.

"What do you want?"

"Who is it, Thomas?"

Agatha's heart was pounding she walked towards the door. Then she saw Rua standing there. She knew who his father was, and like Thomas she did not trust him.

"I need to talk to you."

"Did your father send you here to do his dirty work?" Thomas asked.

Anger flared in Thomas's eyes. He had just about enough of this strange island with dead children and Island Keepers and he wished that he had never set foot on it in the first place. He shut the door and walked back towards the fireside.

"Why can't they leave us alone, Agatha?" he asked.

Rua banged on the door again with his fist. "I won't go away until you let me in!"

Agatha placed her hand on Thomas's shoulder. "Maybe we should hear what he has to say."

"He's Power's son!"

"Please, Thomas, it's a cold night."

"You are too gentle, Agatha – that's your problem."

Thomas walked over and opened the door.

"Just say what you came here to say and go."

Rua stood in front of him and shivered with both fright and cold.

"Can I come inside? If they find me here, they'll kill me."

"Who will kill you?" Agatha cried. She placed her hand over her mouth.

"Come inside, boy," Thomas ordered.

Rua had never been inside the Brennans' cottage before. It was much smaller and more humble than his own sizeable home.

He could smell freshly baked bread and noticed a loaf cooling on a metal rack on the table. His hands were numb with cold, and his lips were blue. Agatha noticed him looking at the bread, so she walked over and cut a slice. Then she buttered it and handed it to him. He ate it hurriedly. Crumbs fell from the corner of his mouth and landed on the floor. He had hardly eaten over the last few days, since the appearance of the children.

"Now sit down, boy̆, and tell us what is bothering you," Agatha said.

Rua finished chewing the piece of bread and sat down on a kitchen chair. The cat jumped up on his lap and nestled its head under his arm.

"I need your help."

"You need our help with what?" Thomas was growing impatient – all he wanted was a peaceful life.

Rua looked at Agatha when he spoke, as Thomas scared him.

"The children."

"How do we know that this isn't a trick and that your father hasn't sent you here?" Thomas snapped.

"Just hear what the boy has to say, Thomas, please." Agatha smiled at Rua. There was something about him that she liked, and she found herself trusting him in spite of who his father was.

Thomas walked to the window and looked out into the yard. A fox walked past. Thomas remembered seeing it before up in the graveyard.

"They are in danger. They're in the house in the Crooked Forest."

"The Witcherly sisters' home? But that's supposed to be haunted!" cried Agatha.

"That is why it's the safest place for them – no-one will ever think of looking for them there."

Thomas began to laugh. "Have you heard yourself, Agatha? You're worried about four ghosts staying in a haunted house?"

"They are children, Thomas." A knot of anger gathered in her stomach like a fist.

"Mrs Brennan is right," said Rua. "Archie, Millie, Ginny and Theo are all children. They all have feelings and eat, drink and sleep like normal children."

"Except that they are not normal children, boy, because they are dead." Thomas was infuriated.

"Believe me when I say that I am as confused as you are," said Rua. "But I think the children's appearance has something to do with the Blood-Red Moon Prophecy."

"This is superstitious nonsense!" Thomas stood up and banged his fist on the table.

The cat jumped off Rua's knee and ran for cover.

"Please, Thomas!"

"Agatha might be an easy target, boy, but I am not," Thomas growled.

Agatha stood up. All the anger that had been simmering inside her since Walter's death spilled out of her mouth like a river bursting a dam.

"Listen to me, Thomas Brennan. I am not an easy

target. I know what I saw and so do you. This boy is talking more sense than you are. So I intend to listen to what he has to say."

A vein throbbed in her temple, and her cheeks were red. She sat down with her back to her husband and locked eyes with Rua.

A small smile crept over Rua's lips. He thought of his own mother and how she never spoke back to his father. She must have had thoughts and opinions, but she buried them the day she married Ezekiel Power.

Agatha took Rua's hand. His fingers were cold.

"What can we do to help them, Rua?"

Thomas was embarrassed by his wife's sudden outburst. Agatha had never spoken to him like that before. Yet, deep down, he liked it.

"They need food and drink," said Rua. "I cannot take food from my house, or my parents will become suspicious."

"Yes, of course, Rua. We'll make sure they get food."

"Thank you, Mrs Brennan." Rua could hardly contain his delight. He leapt up and threw his arms around Agatha's neck. Tears stung his eyes. He was relieved that he did not have to protect the children on his own. "I have to go now or my father will be looking for me."

"Is there anything else we can do?" Agatha's face was flushed. She was shocked by Rua's sudden embrace. Maud Power is a lucky woman to have such a good son, she thought.

"Don't tell anyone I was here."

"That goes without saying," Agatha said reassuringly as she patted Rua on the back. He might have the appearance of a man but he was still a boy.

Thomas walked Rua to the door; then he shook his hand.

"Goodbye, boy," he said.

"Goodbye, Mr Brennan," Rua said as he made his way out into the darkness.

Thomas and Agatha stood in the doorway. Agatha rested her head on Thomas's shoulder, and Thomas placed his arm around Agatha's waist. Together they watched Rua walk away until they could see him no more and then when he disappeared from their sight it was as though he had never existed at all.

Chapter twenty-one

Tread Carefully

Rua stood in the cold, dark hallway. All his family had gone to church. The only sound he could hear was the ticking of the astronomical clock. Its gold face showed the position of the sun and the moon in relation to the earth. It had been in his family for one hundred years. There was the figure of an angel standing guard. A bright red cape was draped around its shoulders and orange flames formed a halo around its head.

On Rua's sixth birthday, Ezekiel had sat him on his knee. Then he told him that on a certain night of a Blood-Red Moon, the angel would strike the face of the clock and the Ghosts of the Wicked Children would be killed by poisoned arrows from the Sacred Bow. Then the ancient prophecy would be reversed, and the islanders would be safe again. Rua didn't know what his father meant until now.

He walked along the hallway and into his parents' bedroom. It was a small room with a low ceiling. It smelt musty. A narrow window allowed a slither of light in, which fell across his parents' metal-framed bed.

Through the window Rua could see the church. Two children in blue coats with silver buttons were playing hide and seek in the churchyard. A tall steeple pierced the clouds. Rua thought of all the families inside the small building, squashed onto uncomfortable benches wearing their Sunday best. Starched shirts that scratched their necks, and shoes that pinched their toes. They would sing hymns from worn-out hymn books and listen while his father told them how they should live their lives. He knew that his father would be angry when he realised that he wasn't there.

He turned back to the bed. Dust motes swam through the air. The green-and-red patchwork blanket that his mother had knitted was folded on a chair by the bed. On it sat her knitting needles. A square patch was added to the blanket on each of the children's birthdays. A wooden crucifix was hung on the wall. Next to it was an oil painting of a blonde girl with her head bent to one side. There was a crown of green flowers on her head and a small gold cross around her neck. She was looking at a blue-and-yellow bird trapped in a cage. The bird's eyes appeared to be glistening in the light. Rua felt sick as he recognised the girl in the painting. It was Ginny. He walked over to it and traced his finger over her face. The painting had been there for as long as Rua could remember but he somehow hadn't thought of it until now. He felt the heat rise in his cheeks and tears gathered in his eyes.

As a young child, he used to imagine that the girl in the painting was alive and the thought occurred to him that he still wished for the same thing. In the bottom right-hand corner, the name Maud Witcherly was painted with black paint followed by the year 1848.

The key to the library was inside a mahogany box with a dove carved into the lid. It sat on a shelf next to the Bible. Rua knew that if anyone opened the library without his father's permission they would be killed. Rua had never even seen his father open it. His fingers trembled as he slid them into the box. The box smelt musty, as though it hadn't been opened in a long time. There was a red-velvet lining that felt smooth under Rua's fingers. There was an inscription stitched into the lining inside the lid in gold thread that read:

Tread carefully on the graves of those that sleep, those little ones with evil hearts.

Rua thought of the graveyard, the iron gate shaped like a heart, the ivy trailing around it. He knew that it all meant something. Then he thought of the ghosts of the Magnificent Children. He would risk anything to save them, even his own life.

He knew that he had to act fast as his parents would

be home from church soon. He had to return the key to the box before they discovered it was missing.

He took hold of the golden key and noticed the heart engraved on it. Then he ran back along the hallway. His parents' wedding photograph hung on the wall – he turned his eyes away from them. He ran past the astronomical clock. For a second he thought that the angel was smiling at him.

He reached the library. His hands were sweaty and his fingers trembled as he fumbled with the lock.

The room was dark inside and it took a moment for his eyes to adjust to the light. He walked over to his father's writing desk which stood in the centre of the room. Then he lit the gas-lamp. The smell of stale tobacco hung in the air. A dog barked in the distance, and Rua jumped with fright.

Then he heard the church bell ring and thought of the people spilling out of the churchyard like bees from a hive. He knew that he didn't have long: they would be home soon.

Rua ran his fingers along the top of the ancient books, some of them hundreds of years old. He picked one off the shelf. Rubies and sapphires formed the shape of a cross on the cover. He glanced quickly inside. The book contained beautiful illustrations of animals. There were birds, snakes, lions and tigers. The words on the pages were written in an old form of the Irish language.

This was not what he was looking for.

Ezekiel strode off ahead of his wife and daughters on the way home after the church service. The wind howled and the crows circled overhead. He kicked a stone across the path and looked up to the sky. The outline of the red moon was already there. The time of the Blood-Red Moon Prophecy was drawing near. He could feel the adrenaline pumping through his veins. He cracked his knuckles, and then pulled a pair of black leather gloves out of his coat pocket and put them on. Thanks to the vigilance of the Island Keepers, he knew that the ghosts of the children were in the Witcherly sisters' home. They were like animals caught in a trap. It was all just as it should be. He thought of his own children and recalled the words of the prophecy:

The children will sleep for one hundred years, then on a night of a Blood-Red Moon they will wake and wander the world as ghosts for the rest of eternity.

The children from the graveyard were not children. He would have to remember that. There was no room for sentimentality. They were the ghosts of children with supernatural abilities. The only way was to reverse the prophecy was to shoot them with a poisoned arrow from the Sacred Bow. When this happened the children would die, the ghosts would disappear forever and the islanders would be safe at last.

His lips felt dry as he walked into the house. He sat

243

down at the kitchen table and drank a glass of water. He could hear the astronomical clock ticking in the hallway. He knew that when the prophecy was reversed the angel would appear and strike the face of the clock and that would signify the end.

He thought of Rua. He was a strong, determined boy, and Ezekiel knew that he would make a good leader for the islanders in years to come. Although he would need to toughen him up. Rua hated the sight of blood, he refused to go hunting with him and would not even kill a rabbit or a bird. Ezekiel knew that all that was about to change. He was sure that Rua was the Chosen One and that he was about to fulfil his destiny. He would be the one to shoot the evil children.

Ezekiel could remember the day that Rua was born, his bright red hair visible as he lay nestled in his mother's arms. He knew then that Rua was destined for greatness.

Rua gazed up at the bookshelves which reached up to the ceiling. In the four corners of the room were gargoyles – dragon-like creatures with their tongues sticking out. Their eyes were made from rubies and emeralds. It was as though they were guarding the books. Rua felt uneasy.

Dust tickled his throat and caused him to sneeze. There was a ladder at the opposite end of the library. Rua climbed it and read the titles of the books:

The Island Keeper's Handbook
Rituals and Observances
Spells and Potions for Godless Children

The books were listed alphabetically. Rua found the books beginning with the letter *B*. Then he looked for a book on *Blood-Red Moon Prophecy*. There wasn't one. But he knew that his father must have one somewhere.

He looked under the letter *S* and took down a book called *Supernatural Children*.

The year *1848* was written down the silver spine, and a red ribbon bookmarked a page. He opened the book and saw a series of illustrations of Ginny, Theo and Archie.

The first one showed Ginny with the blue-and-yellow bird sitting on her tongue. The next illustration was of Theo; his feet were raised off the ground like he was about to fly. The third illustration was of Archie; he was standing in the Crooked Forest beside a fox.

Rua turned the pages, afraid of what he might next see.

Ezekiel heard a noise and knew that he wasn't alone. He took down his rifle from where it hung above the door. He opened the drawer in the wooden dresser and took out three bullets. Then he loaded the gun and walked along the corridor. Although the gun would offer no protection against the ghosts it was all that he had for the moment.

245

Anger swam through his veins. He could not believe that the ghosts had made their way into his home. This was not how it should be: the prophecy could not be fulfilled in this way. He thought of the Sacred Bow and poisoned arrows locked up in a glass case in the secret room in the library. He needed to get the key to the library.

He hurried to his bedroom. The first thing he saw was the mahogany box thrown on the bed. The lid lay on the floor. He picked the box up and to his horror he realised that the key was gone. He flung the box back on the bed, swung around and ran along the hallway.

Rua came to the final illustration. The images he saw were of the islanders brandishing torches, and the children tied to thrones beside a bonfire.

Rua dropped the book on the floor. He could not believe what he had just seen. If the illustrations were right, then the Island Keepers had killed the children one hundred years earlier.

As Rua bent down to pick up the book, he pushed against the bookcase. It began to move. At first he thought that the bookshelf had come loose but then he realized that he had found a secret door. He instinctively knew that the answers he needed lay behind it.

Outside the open library doors Ezekiel could hear someone moving around inside.

He needed to act before Mona and the girls arrived home – they should arrive any minute now.

He stepped inside the library. He noticed a shadow on the floor and saw something move. It looked like a boy. He fired his gun. The shot rang out in the air and the world stopped turning as Ezekiel noticed the boy's red hair. Then he watched him slump forward. A golden key fell from his hand, and blood trickled from his side.

Ezekiel heard the sound of Mona's voice as she ran past him into the library, screaming out the one word he did not want to hear.

"Rua!"

Chapter twenty-two

The Island Keeper's Revenge

Ginny sat on the swing that hung from the crooked oak tree outside the Witcherly sisters' house. The bough of the tree sighed under the weight of her body and the sunlight shone through the pale green leaves of the tree which were wet with dew. Ginny sat back on the swing. She pushed off with her left foot against the worn patch of grass until the swing began to move. Then she swung higher and higher through the air.

She closed her eyes tight and imagined that she was flying. She could feel the gentle warmth from the buttery yellow sun on her skin. The breeze ruffled her hair. Her fingernails gripped the weather-beaten rope.

She thought of Rua, his red hair and his pale skin. She realised that he was a true friend to her and she was glad that she had met him. She knew that they could trust him even if Theo didn't.

Ginny felt the wind on her face and found it hard to believe that she was one hundred and thirteen years old. She did not know how it was possible to be dead and to feel so alive.

The house looked different as she moved through the air. Ginny noticed that the red paint was chipped on the windowsill and that a sparrow had built a nest with sticks. Three chicks sat with their necks stretched and their tiny beaks open wide. Their mother regurgitated the body of a worm into their open mouths. The glass on the windows appeared glossy. Ginny could see shadows moving in the dark inside. They were the shadows of Theo and Archie. As she swung higher she could see the mountain: it appeared red and black like a bad apple.

Beyond the mountain, she could see the green sea. It wound its way around the shore like a serpent. Then Ginny remembered a boat and shiny black leeches covering Millie's body. They were sucking her blood. Ginny was there too and she was dancing. Twirling around and around while a man played the violin.

Suddenly the sky and the ground merged. Ginny felt as though the world had swallowed her whole and then spat her out like a sour grape. She was thrown into the air. Her head hit the ground first and she heard her skull split against a jagged rock. It sounded like an egg being cracked open against the corner of a pan. Blood glistened on the ground and the swing moved above her. The crooked tree bent over her. It stretched spindly branches down towards her. The sky turned grey. The early morning sun hid its yellow face behind grey clouds and then raindrops fell on her skin. It felt as though the sky was crying. Ginny thought of the birds in the nest and Blue trapped inside her body, in a cage made of bones. Ginny coughed hard and her ribs ached as Blue flew out of her mouth.

"Fly away, Blue," Ginny muttered, her voice sounding gravelly.

Then there was a sound. A gunshot pinged through the air.

"*Rua!*" Ginny cried.

Instinctively she knew that he had been shot. She stretched her fingers out and clawed at the grass. The smell of the damp earth filled her nostrils. Then rain pounded against her skin as blood trickled down her head. Her dress was wet, her hair was tangled and matted with blood and dead leaves. She crawled up to the back door of the house and sobbed into the wet ground.

Theo heard the shot too. He was in the bedroom alone, sitting on the dapple-grey rocking horse.

He had been watching shards of bone falling like snow in the water-filled snow globe and studying the miniature figures, each one a perfectly formed version of Ginny, Millie, Archie and himself. Suddenly he'd thrown the snow globe violently against the wooden beam and watched the pieces of bone and shards of glass fall to the ground. He'd picked up the miniature figure of Ginny and cut his finger on a splinter of glass. Dark-red blood had bubbled on the surface of his skin and transferred onto the figurine.

When the gunshot was fired, Theo thrust the figure into his pocket. His face crumpled like a piece of discarded litter as he thought of Ginny. He hadn't seen her for hours. She said that she was going to the graveyard. He ran to the window and pressed his face against the glass. However, all he could see was the old wooden swing moving back and forth. He ran down the stairs, two at a time, overwhelmed with panic and fear. Beads of perspiration gathered like knots in cotton on his forehead. Thoughts of Ginny tumbled through his distraught mind. He had known that they were wrong to trust Rua. He blinked his tears away and prayed that his dear Ginny hadn't been shot.

Archie and Millie were in the kitchen when Theo burst in. He saw Ginny lying on the wooden table, her arms outstretched. Blood seeped from a cut that like looked like a red seam on her head.

Theo ran over to her and held her in his arms. He was relieved to see that there was just a small cut on her head – there was no way that it had been made with a gunshot. Ginny leant into him and sobbed into his shoulder. Her blood stained his shirt but he did not care.

Archie lit the gas-lamp, and checked that the door was latched.

"I heard the gunshot, Ginny – I thought they got you," said Theo.

Her swollen eyelids were like black slits, her blue eyes barely visible beneath them.

"It's Rua. I think he's been shot."

Theo pulled away from Ginny. He noticed that she was wearing Rua's green coat. Theo didn't trust Rua, he felt as though he was taking advantage of Ginny's good nature. Rua's father was an Island Keeper and for all he knew Rua could be leading them into a trap.

"Why should I care if he's been shot?" His finger throbbed from when he cut it on the shard of glass. He placed it in his mouth and sucked the blood. He could not believe that he could still bleed even though he was dead.

"Because he was trying to help us!" Ginny cried through her tears.

Millie filled a brown bowl with water. Then she found an old rag in the cupboard. It was beside a silver spoon and a chipped cup. She wet the cloth and dabbed Ginny's head. Then Millie swirled the rag in the water. It made a gentle splashing sound as it turned red. The colour of Ginny's blood. A line of concentration appeared on Millie's brow as she picked tiny grey stones out of Ginny's forehead.

"That hurts!" Ginny gasped. Her head stung. She gripped the edge of the table and curled her toes.

"I'm sorry, Ginny, just one more." Millie pulled out the last stone with her fingernail. The bleeding had almost stopped. Then she lined up the tiny grey stones like silver bullets on the windowsill.

"I have to go," Ginny said.

She carefully stepped down from the table. Her leg hurt too. As she hobbled over to the door she looked down. There was a hole in her dress and a dark-red graze on her knee.

"Where are you going, Ginny?" Millie cried.

"I have to see if Rua is all right. He was going to his father's library, to see if he could find anything that could help us." She turned and cupped Millie's face in her hands. "Thank you, Millie. You're a good child."

Millie blushed. She was glad that she could help Ginny. She had a feeling that Ginny had been good to her in the past.

Theo stormed out of the kitchen, banging the door behind him. He was angry with Ginny for caring so much about Rua. It felt as though she was betraying him.

Ginny walked out of the house and closed the door behind her. The rain had stopped, but the wind howled. She pulled Rua's green hood up over her head and stuffed her hands into the pockets. She felt something there, beside a piece of fluff. It was a small silver medal with the picture of a saint on it: a woman with a halo above her head holding a rose. Ginny imagined Rua placing his hand into the pocket and rubbing his fingers over the medal. She hoped that he was all right. As she walked past the swing she noticed her blood on a patch of grass. A robin redbreast hopped onto a rock and spread its wings as though it was about to take flight.

As Ginny got deeper into the Crooked Forest, she could hear a rustling in the leaves. She turned back to look at the house. The light from the kitchen window was barely visible through the trees. Ginny wondered if she was being followed. Perhaps the person who had fired the gun had come looking for her too. Then she remembered Rua's words. He had said that the Island Keepers were afraid of the Crooked Forest and the Witcherly sisters' home. She tried to run, but her leg was too painful. She could smell something peculiar like lemons and oranges. She turned quickly and thought that she saw a woman with red hair, wearing a pink tutu and a bodice covered in pearls, dart in behind one of the trees. Ginny decided that her mind was playing tricks on her and kept walking.

When she reached the edge of the forest, the road stretched out before her like a piece of string. She could see trails of black smoke coming from the chimneys and yellow lights illuminating the windows of houses in the village.

Ginny walked along the road. There were muddy fields on either side of stone walls. She held onto the wall for support. Puddles had formed on the ground. She was careful to avoid them. She looked ahead and saw the church with its large steeple pointing up towards the sky.

Nestled in the shadow of the church was a house with a slanted roof. A group of people had gathered outside.

Ginny saw a gap in the stone wall. She darted through it into a field and then, bent low, moved cautiously along behind the wall until she was much closer to the house by the church. Now she could see everything clearly through the gaps between the stones that formed the wall.

The faces of the people were sombre and their clothes were black. Ginny saw that a hearse had pulled up outside the house. The people bowed their heads and waited outside as four men carried a wooden coffin in through the front door. Then Ginny saw a priest arrive. He had a Bible in his hands and he placed his hand on the shoulder of a small woman as he bent his head and spoke to her. Ginny knew from her black dress that she was in mourning. Two pencil-thin women stood on either side of her, linking her arms as she cried. Ginny thought that if the thin women were to move away the mourning woman would collapse, like a deck of cards. A lace veil covered her eyes. Then Ginny noticed tendrils of bright red hair escaping from under the woman's black hat. Hair the same colour as Rua's. Ginny pressed her fingers to her lips to prevent a cry from escaping as she realised that the woman was Rua's mother.

A man stepped out of the house. He was a tall man with a black beard and a large nose.

"A tragedy has taken place inside my house today. My youngest son Rua was killed."

Ezekiel bent his head towards the ground and stared at his boots. Tears sat like boulders at the back of his throat. He was in shock; he could not believe that he had killed his son.

"We all know who was responsible for this act!" a man with a wooden leg shouted.

Ezekiel held up his left hand to silence him.

"It was those evil children!" an old woman with a hump on her back and a patch over her left eye shouted.

"I came home from doing the Lord's work and found one of them with my rifle," said Ezekiel. "My boy Rua was lying in a pool of his own blood. I chased after the boy but he escaped out of the window." His face puckered up and two large tears slid down his cheeks.

The crowd were stunned by his sudden outburst of grief.

A young woman with black eyes and a baby resting on her left hip shouted out: "*Let's stop those evil children once and for all!*"

The crowd cheered.

Ezekiel stepped into the house and shut the door.

Ginny knew that she had no time to waste. She had to get back to the house to warn the others that the Island Keepers were on their way. It would only be a matter of time before they caught up with them.

She hurried back along the stone wall and out onto the road. Then she walked back up the path towards the forest. Her heart thumped and her head hurt. A seagull squawked above her.

Ginny could not believe that Rua was dead. She blamed herself. Blood trickled down her cheek and mingled with her tears. She walked quickly towards the forest, desperate for the crooked trees to cover her with their branches. Her mind was racing. Why had she let Rua risk his life to help them? She wished that they had never met. At least he would still be alive.

Inside the forest, darkness covered her like a cloak. She felt at home amongst the wild animals – the foxes and badgers and the insects that crawled around inside the belly of the earth. She heard a branch snap and knew that she wasn't alone.

She scurried along until she could see the Witcherlys' house ahead of her. Leaves crunched and she turned her head and saw a man behind her. She screamed and tried to run away but she tripped over a rock that was covered in dank green moss. Her ankle twisted as she fell. The man loomed over her as she screamed.

Chapter twenty-three

Away They Flew

Agatha paced the cottage floor, she had grown impatient waiting for Thomas to return and she knew that something bad was going to happen. She'd had the same sick feeling in the pit of her stomach on the day that she received the telegram from the War Office saying that Walter had been killed in action.

A blue vase sat on the wooden dresser next to a brown serving tray with oval-shaped handles. The image of a cotton mill was painted on the tray, but the paint was chipped.

Agatha picked up the vase. Her sister had given it to her on the day of Walter's funeral. It seemed as though everything she owned was tainted with sadness. The vase contained yellowing holly leaves. Agatha felt the prickly leaves. The bright red berries had shrivelled up and turned brown. Everything dies in the end, Agatha thought, then she peered through the window.

There was a small crack in the glass she hadn't noticed before. The snow had melted and in a strange way she missed it. The red fox walked along the path and sat outside the cottage door as it had done every night since the blood-red moon appeared. Agatha wondered why it had chosen to visit her. In a way, it made her feel special. She thought that when the moon returned to its usual milky-white colour the fox would disappear. This worried her much more than it should have. Agatha felt as though the fox was her only friend.

She emptied the remains of her dinner into a metal saucepan with a broken handle – some stew – scraps of meat, carrots and potatoes and a crust of brown bread.

Agatha went outside to the animal and placed the saucepan on the ground. The breeze blew down her neck and along her spine. The fox ate quickly and then walked straight past Agatha and in through the open door. Its snow-white paws looked yellow and its nails brittle, but its red coat glistened. The fox's black eyes reminded Agatha of currants in a loaf of bread. Stan arched his back and then walked away, the way that cats do when they feel threatened.

"Ghosts and foxes, whatever next?" Agatha asked

herself as she watched the fox curl up in front of the fire as if it belonged there.

Agatha sat down in the old armchair. A spring jutted out underneath. She picked up a ball of red wool and her knitting needles – she had decided to knit a scarf for Archie. It was the same colour as his coat.

The sound of a girl screaming came from outside the cottage door. The fox ran and hid under the table. Agatha picked up a knife from the dresser and her hands trembled as the front door flew open.

"Aggie, it's me!"

Agatha dropped the knife to the ground. She was relieved to hear Thomas's voice. The wind followed Thomas into the cottage. He was holding a screaming girl in his arms. She had a pale face, long blonde hair and her eyes were like blue whirlpools. Agatha noticed a sprinkling of freckles on the bridge of her nose. Her head was bleeding and blood dripped down her cheek and onto her blue dress which was torn. She was wearing a green coat. In the hollow of her neck sat a small gold cross, and a blue vein was visible beneath her skin. She reminded Agatha of Archie. The girl was screaming at the top of her lungs like a wild animal caught in a trap. Agatha noticed that Thomas's hand was bleeding from where the girl had slit his skin with her sharp fingernails. Agatha knew that she was one of the children from the graveyard.

"Thomas, what are you doing? Did anyone see you bringing her here?"

"I don't know."

"You don't know?"

"I don't think so."

"Did you hurt her?"

"Of course not."

"She's bleeding."

"I found her like that, in the Crooked Forest."

Thomas let go of the girl, and she fell to the floor on her knees. Then she bent over and coughed.

"Thomas, get the girl some water quickly."

As Agatha bent over the girl, a small bird darted out of her mouth and flew around the room.

Thomas dropped the glass onto the floor. It broke into a hundred pieces. The light from the fire made the shards of glass sparkle like diamonds.

"For heaven's sake, Thomas!" said Agatha.

"Why did you bring me here?" the girl gasped. "I have to go to warn the others."

As she spoke, Agatha recognised her English accent.

"You can't go anywhere in your condition."

Agatha helped her over to the armchair. She tossed her knitting onto the floor, to make room for her.

"Sit down, girl," she ordered.

"I need to go!" the girl pleaded.

"What's your name, girl?"

"Ginny. Please let me go!"

Agatha walked over to her husband. She could tell by the look on his face that something bad had happened.

"What's wrong, Thomas? You're as nervous as a kitten."

"It's the boy, Aggie."

"Archie? Please don't tell me they have hurt him!"

"No, Agatha, it's not Archie. It's Rua. Ezekiel Power's boy."

"Rua's dead!" Ginny blurted out.

"Oh God, no!" Agatha walked over to the Holy Water font that hung on the wall by the door. She dipped her fingers into the water and blessed herself. Then she walked over to the kitchen table and sat down. A yellow holly leaf fell from the vase. Agatha rubbed it between her fingers. It felt soft, like a piece of wet velvet between her finger and thumb.

The moon shone in through the window and the cuckoo-clock ticked on the mantelpiece.

"How did it happen?" Agatha asked.

"He was shot in the chest," Thomas replied.

"By whom?" Agatha gasped.

Thomas shook his head and didn't answer.

Agatha walked over to Ginny and placed her hand on her head. Then she knelt down and looked into her eyes.

"We promised Rua that we would help you," she

said, "and that is what we intend to do."

"They think we shot him, but we would never do that!"

Blue flew over and perched on the back of Ginny's chair as she sobbed.

"It will be all right, I promise," came a child's voice.

Ginny, Agatha and Thomas were confused as they could not tell where the voice was coming from.

Millie stepped out from under the kitchen table. Her dress was creased, and her eyes and nose were still black. It took a moment for them to return to normal.

"Did you know she was here, Aggie?" Thomas inquired as he studied the little girl.

"Are you the fox?" Agatha said.

Millie nodded, and Agatha smiled. Thomas shook his head in disbelief.

The sound of dogs barking outside the door alerted them to danger. Agatha looked out the window. A crowd of Island Keepers were heading towards the cottage. They were brandishing torches. Orange flames danced in the air.

"They are coming for us!" Millie cried.

Agatha ran over to Ginny as Thomas reached for his shotgun. He used it for hunting rabbits. Blue sensed danger and flew back into Ginny's mouth.

"We have to leave now!" Ginny cried. She pulled Millie towards the door.

"Wait! You can't go out that way – they'll see you," Agatha said.

"Is there another way out?" Ginny asked. Her head had stopped bleeding but her face looked so pale that Agatha thought she might faint.

"Go to Archie's room – Millie, show her where it is – and climb out the window. Then make your way up through the Crooked Forest and back to the house."

Two gunshots were fired outside and they pinged off the chimney.

"Thomas will stall them!" Agatha shouted after the girls.

"Out you come, Brennan! We know you're in there!" Ezekiel Power ordered.

Thomas knew that Ezekiel was grieving for his son, and he was out for revenge. Just like he himself was when Walter died. In his frame of mind, he would kill anyone: he was blood-hungry. Thomas loaded his shotgun. He placed the gun on the table then he slowly opened the door.

Agatha walked over to the dresser and picked up the photograph of Walter. He looked so handsome in his uniform.

"I couldn't protect you, Walter, but maybe I can help them."

In the bedroom Ginny felt very weak. Pain ripped through her body.

There was a small window in the front wall of the

room and another at the far side. A chair, a small wooden bed and a wardrobe were the only furniture

Millie ran over to the back window, unhooked the latch and wrenched the sash open. A draught blew around the room, and the orange curtains which framed the window billowed in the breeze.

"Come on, Ginny!" Millie cried.

"Wait a minute." Ginny opened the front window a crack – she wanted to hear what they were saying outside. She cautiously peered out.

She saw Ezekiel step forward and look Thomas Brennan square in the eye. Grief was etched on his face.

"I don't want any trouble, Ezekiel," Thomas said.

"Did you hear that? He doesn't want any trouble," Ezekiel mocked Thomas. Then he turned to face the angry crowd.

"*Burn his house down!*" one man shouted.

"*He is helping those evil children!*" another yelled.

"Hush now, people," Ezekiel said. Anger flashed in his eyes and his voice was shaky. "My boy Rua died tonight."

"Sorry for your trouble," Thomas said, bowing his head.

"Sorry, are you?"

"I had nothing to do with it, and neither did those children."

"*He's defending them!*" a man with red hair shouted.

"You had something to do with it all right." Ezekiel

moved close to Thomas. "You were hiding someone or something that night we visited your cottage, I know you were."

Agatha appeared in the doorway with the shotgun in her hands. Her hair was loose and blew like a halo around her head.

"Get off our property, you are trespassing," she said.

"Agatha, put the gun down," Thomas pleaded.

"Listen to your husband, Mrs Brennan, and put the gun down," Ezekiel ordered.

Ginny moved away from the window and across the wooden floor. Her mind was spinning, and her bottom lip quivered like a loose branch on a tree. The realisation that Rua had died suddenly hit her. How could she have let that happen? She shouldn't have allowed him to get close to her. Precious Rua was dead.

The islanders were right: they were evil children. She was a wicked girl.

The men's voices grew louder. Millie and Ginny realised that they were inside the house. They didn't have any time to lose.

"Ginny, please hurry!" Millie pleaded. Her eyes were wide with fear. She was halfway out of the window. It would have been so easy for her to go and leave Ginny behind, but that was something she would never do.

Ginny looked over at Millie. Her pale skin appeared clammy, and her eyelid was twitching. Ginny knew that she had to go for her sake.

"Come quickly!" Millie said as she climbed out of the window. The curtains followed her outside into the darkness.

Ginny climbed onto the windowsill.

The door handle turned, and Ezekiel entered the room.

"*Run!*" screamed Agatha.

Ginny jumped out of the window before Ezekiel could catch her.

Outside, Ginny took Millie's hand, and they ran. Faster than they had ever run before. Millie let go of Ginny's hand, and shapeshifted into a fox. Then together they jumped over the broken wooden fence at the back of the house, past the thorny rose bushes and the bare apple trees. Then they ran through the small stream, mud splattering on Ginny's dress and squelching underfoot. A toad with a head like a knuckle sat on a triangular-shaped rock and stuck out his tongue as they passed by. They kept going until they came to the edge of the forest. They did not look back once. The wind blew through Ginny's silver-blonde hair, and raindrops tumbled from the sky.

Then the Witcherly sisters' home appeared like a vision. Candlelight illuminated the windows which looked like eyes watching as they approached. Ginny prepared herself as she knew that the worst was yet to come.

Millie burst into the house with Ginny right behind her. They found Theo and Archie sitting at the kitchen table. The back door had blown open in the wind and Ginny banged it shut. Theo and Archie both jumped up.

"What's wrong?" Theo asked as he gazed into Ginny's bloodshot eyes.

Tears streamed down her cheeks as she sat on the rocking chair and took a moment to catch her breath.

"Rua's dead," she sobbed.

Theo walked over to the corner of the room. He felt as though he was suffocating.

"Do the Island Keepers know where we are?" he asked.

"Rua's dead, Theo, don't you care?" Ginny said.

"There is nothing we can do about Rua. We have to protect ourselves."

"How?" Millie asked.

Archie walked over to his sister and hugged her. He could feel her bones rattling beneath the thin material of her dress.

Ginny stood up and walked over to the window. The swing on the oak tree was moving, although no-one was on it. In the distance, she could make out the light from the Island Keepers' torches as they flickered. She knew that they would arrive soon.

She turned to Theo.

"Theo, I want you to show me how I died."

"What do you mean?" Theo was bewildered.

"Theo, you have a gift for seeing how people are going to die."

"How do you know this?"

"I am not sure how I know. I remember it somehow."

"You're being ridiculous – if we're already dead how can I show you how you're going to die? And we have to leave right now!"

"Please, Theo, show me how I died. I want to know if I can die twice."

The children heard the gate open, then the sound of footsteps on the path and fists pounding on the door.

"Hurry, Theo, please!" Ginny cried.

Millie turned to Archie and spoke to him using her mind. The children did not understand why Ginny was behaving this way at this moment in time.

Theo shut his eyes tight and tried to concentrate. He could not remember having this gift, but using it felt as natural to him as breathing.

The front door flew open. Theo's eyelids flickered and his eyes became as large as dinner plates. Two of the Island Keepers ran into the kitchen and they saw in an image projected in the air how Genevieve Potter was murdered by the Witcherly sisters in 1848.

Chapter twenty-four

A Ghost Is Born

Rua woke up alone. Candles flickered in the room. A black sheet had been placed over his face. He pulled it off and sat up gasping for air.

The blood-red moon shone in through the window. A red cross had been painted on the inside of the bedroom door. Rua felt liquid trickling from his side. He looked down and saw a hole in his chest. A puddle of blood had gathered beside his bed. He felt dizzy and went to stand up, but slipped in the blood and fell to the ground.

Then memories flashed before his eyes. Ginny in the graveyard, her lips pressed against his, the prophecy, the library and his father's gun, then the gunshot. He knew he had to help Ginny and the children. He hoped he wasn't too late.

He tore a section from the black sheet and tied it around his chest to stem the bleeding. Then he stumbled out of the room.

It seemed like a long walk down the hallway to the library. He placed his hand on the wall to steady himself and walked past the astronomical clock. The library door was locked. Rua stumbled into his parents' bedroom and saw that his father had placed the mahogany box containing the key back on the shelf. He reached for it and a pain seared through his side as he opened the lid. Then he took the key out. The red-velvet lining inside the box matched the colour of the blood that trickled from his body.

He walked back along the corridor, clasping his hand over his wound. Then he placed the key in the lock, opened the door and went inside. There were spots of blood on the floorboards. Rua lit the gas-lamp on his father's desk. He picked it up and walked over to the bookcase. He pressed his hand against it and felt relieved when it opened.

Inside he found a small room. The walls were decorated in wallpaper with images of children on it. Some of them were flying. There was a fox and a boy without a head. A girl had no eyes, nose or mouth. In the middle of the scene was Ginny. She was there staring at him from the wallpaper. In her hand was a birdcage that looked as though it was made from bone. A beautiful bird was trapped inside.

There was a table in the centre of the room. It was covered with a lace tablecloth. In a glass case was a bow and some arrows. Resting on the table beside the glass case was an ancient book bound in red leather. It smelt old and musty. The pages were decorated with gold leaf. Rua opened the book; it felt heavy in his hands. The title was written inside the cover: *The Blood-Red Moon Prophecy – 1848. Badblood.*

Rua slid down onto the floor. The bleeding had stopped now, and he did not feel any pain despite the size of the wound. He turned the pages slowly to ensure that he did not miss anything. Rua knew that the red leather book contained the answers that he was looking for about the ghosts of the Magnificent Children. He had promised them that he would take care of them and he had meant it.

He read the prophecy twice, trying to make sense of it.

The children will sleep for one hundred years, then on a night of a Blood-Red Moon they will wake and wander the world as ghosts for the rest of eternity.

Then he continued to read the book until he came to a section written in red ink. It was headed: *How to Reverse the Prophecy and Kill the Ghosts Forever.*

With a gathering feeling of dread, he began to read. At first he thought he was mistaken but, as the words began to sink in, he threw the book across the room and screamed like an animal caught in a trap.

He prayed that he wasn't too late to save Ginny, Theo, Millie and Archie from his father and the Island Keepers' attack.

Chapter twenty-five

The Golden Sun

Rua hid behind a crooked oak tree at the bottom of the
mountain as the children were led in a procession by
the Island Keepers towards the graveyard at the top.
He was so close to Ginny that he could almost have
touched her as she went past. She looked so alive, her
pale skin shimmering under the moonlight. Her hands
were bound behind her back with thick red rope.
Millie was behind her, hands also tied. Rua could see
the head of a small doll peeping out above the frills at
the top of Millie's pinafore. He guessed that she had
taken it from the Witcherly sisters' house. He could see
the fear in Millie's eyes and wondered how people
could be so cruel. He knew she was a ghost but she
was a little girl too, a little girl who liked to play with
dolls. Rua knew that it would only be a matter of time

before the ceremony would take place. Then the prophecy would be reversed and the children would be laid to rest forever.

Rua was a ghost now too. He could not be sure how this had happened but suspected it had something to do with the prophecy. There was no going back: his future, whatever that might be, lay with Ginny, Theo, Archie and Millie.

His heart ached as he thought of leaving his mother and his brother and sisters behind.

Ever since he was a child, Rua wondered why his father cared so much about the Blood-Red Moon Prophecy and guarding the secrets that it held. Now he was beginning to understand, although his father had got it all wrong. The children were not a threat to the people on the island. It was the other way around.

As he ran past Gravedigger's Cottage he noticed that the front door was open. He wondered if Thomas and Agatha had been captured too, so he quickly peered inside and saw that their furniture was broken. He realised in horror that the islanders had taken their anger out on them. The gravedigger's shovel was broken in half outside the door.

He ran through the crooked trees and up the mountain behind the procession. The silver leaves quivered in the breeze as he ran along the narrow path.

Suddenly, before him, he saw thousands of fireflies beating their wings, their bright bodies illuminating the night. He looked closer and saw that they had formed the shape of a circus tent.

A beautiful woman, wearing a pink ballet tutu and a bodice embroidered with pearls, went by on the back of a sauntering elephant. She stopped in front of Rua.

"Look after her for me, treasure!" she cried, then she saluted him and somersaulted through the air.

Rua heard the sound of people clapping and cheering. He looked up at the trees. Each of the leaves had become a person's face and they were all smiling down at him. A tiger roared and ran towards Rua. He closed his eyes and when he opened them the tiger was gone – instead, he saw a thin man whose face looked like the moon, playing a sad tune on a violin.

Two slim women with shiny black hair and red lips emerged from beneath a weeping-willow tree. Their faces were covered with white face powder, and they shared one body between them. They had blue silk shoes on their feet. They held green fans in front of their eyes, which were decorated with birds of paradise. Rua realised that the island was full of ghosts.

When he neared the top of the mountain Rua saw the largest bonfire he had ever seen. It was outside the graveyard and crowds of people had gathered there. It seemed that all the islanders were there to witness the reversal of the prophecy and he hoped that he wasn't too late. He ran up the last stretch of the mountain, barely pausing to catch his breath. He placed his hand on his chest and realised that it had healed – there wasn't even a scratch there. The bullet hole had disappeared.

The orange flames from the bonfire reached up into the sky. Rua realised that he could not get close to the bonfire now, because of all the people that had converged. The only way he could get close to the ghosts of the Magnificent Children was to take a shortcut through the graveyard. He pushed open the heart-shaped iron gate and stepped inside. Then he ran between the headstones and the open graves. An owl with yellow eyes sat on the stone wall, watching everything.

Rua remembered the last time in the graveyard with Ginny. He had promised to help her and he would not let her down. He climbed onto the wall and noticed Ginny first. Her hands were tied behind her back and her long blonde hair blew across her face. Tears stained her cheeks.

His father stood in front of her brandishing a bow and arrow.

Behind Ginny the other children were lined up, their hands tied behind their backs, probably in the order that Ezekiel was going to shoot them: Ginny, Theo, Archie and Millie. No doubt he planned to throw them onto the bonfire when the prophecy was reversed.

"*Kill them, kill them!*" the hostile crowd shouted.

Ezekiel raised his left hand, clutching the Sacred

Bow and poisoned arrows, above his head. "Silence, all of you!" he ordered and the angry crowd obeyed him.

Even the breeze hushed. Only the flames defied him and continued to hiss and crack.

"What has happened here on this island was foretold in the ancient prophecy. My precious son Rua was born to reverse it and to kill those evil ghosts once and for all. However, he himself has been killed by these wicked children. Therefore, it is my duty as his father, as well as your Preacher and the Protector of Souls on this island, to take on this arduous task myself."

Rua could not believe what he was hearing: it was his father who killed him, not the children.

Rua thought of the words of the prophecy and what he had read about its reversal. He concentrated as hard as he possibly could. He thought of the astronomical clock and the hands of time moving slowly, effortlessly forward and the angel ringing the bell.

"*Rua is alive!*" someone shouted from the crowd.

All the faces turned to look at him, including his father's.

An astonished smile flickered across Ezekiel's lips as he realised that his son was alive. Then it turned to anguish as Rua leapt off the wall and wrestled him to the ground. Ezekiel dropped the bow and arrow and the Island Keepers formed a circle around the father and son as they fought.

A huge smile broke across Ginny's face when she saw Rua. She coughed and Blue flew out of her mouth.

"Rua!" his mother cried in disbelief. She thought she was seeing things.

Ezekiel was a strong man and Rua was no match for him. He picked Rua up and smashed him face down on the ground. Then he picked up a rock and drew back, raising the rock over his head. But he didn't hit Rua with it. He hesitated then dropped the rock onto the ground.

Rua lay there trying to catch his breath. He saw blood on the ground, his blood, and felt a pain searing through his entire body. He realised that his head was bleeding and his left eye-socket throbbed too. He turned over onto his back and looked up at his father who had picked up the bow and arrow.

Then Ezekiel bent down and pressed the arrow against Rua's chest.

"You are not my son any more!" he growled.

Rua had never seen his father like this before.

"No, Ezekiel!" Mona screamed.

Rua turned his head to look at her. Her face was distorted with anger and grief as she ran towards her husband and son.

Rua shut his eyes and waited for the arrow to strike.

There was a sudden silence.

Rua opened his eyes.

Everything had stopped moving. Time had stood still.

Rua stood up and looked around him. All of the Island Keepers were as still as statues, as was the crowd. The flames of the bonfire, which had danced in the darkness only moments earlier, stood in an otherworldly way, forming the shape of a heart.

Rua took the bow and arrow from his father's hand and threw them into the fire.

Then he went to his mother, who was motionless. As he kissed her on the cheek, he heard Millie's voice.

"Rua, untie us!"

"Hurry, Rua!" Ginny cried.

Her anguished expression told him that there was no time to lose.

Rua quickly untied all their hands.

Millie started to cry and Archie placed his arm around her protectively.

"Let's go!" ordered Theo who sensed that time could not stay frozen for much longer.

"Wait," Rua replied. Then he took Ginny in his arms and hugged her.

"We thought you were dead!" Ginny cried in disbelief.

"I am dead," said Rua. And he smiled at her.

"Hurry!" called Theo.

They ran down the mountainside as fast as they could, the red moon guiding them in the darkness.

When they reached Thomas and Agatha's cottage at

the bottom of the mountain, Archie ran inside. Stan the cat was stretched out on the rug in front of the fire. But all the furniture in the kitchen was broken up, and Archie feared the worst.

He ran into their bedroom but it was empty. Here, too, everything was wrecked. Where were Thomas and Agatha? Had they run away? Or been taken away by force? Were they dead?

But then, in his bedroom, he found them lying together on his small bed. They looked as though they were sleeping although he could not be sure. Perhaps they were dead. He had no way of knowing as time had stood still. But he believed they were alive.

Agatha had Walter's photograph in her hand. Archie stared hard at the photo and memorised Walter's face, just in case he should meet him along the way. Then he kissed each of them on the head and walked into the kitchen.

He took their wedding photograph so that he had something to remember them by. He hoped they wouldn't mind. In return he took off his red coat and left it on the kitchen chair.

"Thank you, Agatha. If I ever meet Walter, I will tell him how kind you were to me."

Then he walked out of the cottage with a heavy heart. He hated to leave Thomas and Agatha behind. He remembered how Thomas had carried him on his back and how Agatha had bathed him and put him to bed. In many ways, she had been kinder to him than his own mother ever had.

Archie ran towards the beach.

"Hurry!" shouted Ginny.

She was standing on the shore, the waves lapping against her ankles. Theo and Rua pushed the boat out into the water. Millie was sitting in it, holding the doll from the Witcherly sisters' home. Archie ran towards them and Ginny helped him on board.

The children looked towards the mountain and at the wooden cross that marked the graveyard. The flames on the bonfire started to flicker, and they realised that the hands of time had begun to move again.

Archie saw Thomas and Agatha running out of the door of the cottage and towards the shore. Agatha was holding his red coat in her hands.

"Archie, I love you!" cried Agatha.

"I love you too!" Archie shouted back. Tears flowed down his cheeks, and Millie held her brother tight as he sobbed into her hair.

The blood-red moon slipped away and sunlight erupted on the horizon, golden and beautiful, and with it came the promise of hope. Hope for the Ghosts of Magnificent Children as their journey had only just begun.

The End

Exclusive

Coming 2017

The Girl Who Ate the Stars

Caroline Busher

Prologue

The Girl Who Ate The Stars

It is the dead of night. A pack of hungry wolves howls outside Ravenskull Castle. Lottie is woken from her sleep. She creeps from her bed and goes outside. Leaves crunch beneath her feet as she enters the Forest of Non-Existence. She sees a wolf with teeth as sharp as needles and fangs as red as blood. A waterfall of children's tears flows over the edge of a glass mountain.

A girl called Cuán, who has two hearts and eats the stars, sleeps in the hollow of a tree made from bone. The sky is black. Cuán wakes from her sleep and moves towards Lottie like a starving beast. She has claws like daggers and sapphire eyes shaped like half-moons. Her dress is made from the petals of black roses and she wears a necklace made of thorns.

An ill wind blows and a pack of bloodthirsty wolves

suddenly appears. They howl and pace back and forth, their amber eyes gleaming like gems in the darkness.

The petals from Cuán's dress fall to the ground to reveal the body a Wolf Girl. She drops to her knees and growls, the transformation complete. The thorns around her neck dig into her thick fur. She reaches out her claw and the pack of wolves whimper and tremble with fright. They retreat into the forest.

Lottie does not fear her strange companion. She stares into her sapphire eyes and for a moment she thinks that they are made of stars.